*Disney*

# Scary

## Storybook Collection

DISNEP PRESS

LOS ANGELES • NEW YORK

# Contents

**Peter Pan**
The Curse of the Crow . . . . . . . . . . . . . . . . . . . . . . . . . . 1

**Inside Out**
Riley's Haunted Halloween . . . . . . . . . . . . . . . . . . 17

**Big Hero 6**
Lights Out! . . . . . . . . . . . . . . . . . . . . . . . . . . . . . . . . 35

**Winnie the Pooh**
Frankenpooh . . . . . . . . . . . . . . . . . . . . . . . . . . . . . . 51

**The Jungle Book**
Shadows in the Jungle . . . . . . . . . . . . . . . . . . . . . . 67

**Finding Nemo**
The Ghost-Light Fish . . . . . . . . . . . . . . . . . . . . . . . 85

**101 Dalmatians**
Detective Lucky . . . . . . . . . . . . . . . . . . . . . . . . . . 101

**Beauty and the Beast**
Belle's Mysterious Message . . . . . . . . . . . . . . . . 117

**Toy Story**
Toy Story of Terror! . . . . . . . . . . . . . . . . . . . . . . . 133

**Alice in Wonderland**
Queen of Frights . . . . . . . . . . . . . . 151

**Mickey & Friends**
Mickey's Slumber Party . . . . . . . . . . . 169

**Brave**
Merida's Wild Ride . . . . . . . . . . . . . 187

**The Lion King**
A Dark and Scar-y Night . . . . . . . . . . 203

**Wreck-It Ralph**
Power Outage! . . . . . . . . . . . . . . . 219

**Snow White and the Seven Dwarfs**
The Queen's Spell . . . . . . . . . . . . . . 235

**Sleeping Beauty**
A Message for Maleficent . . . . . . . . . . 251

**Up**
One Brave Dug . . . . . . . . . . . . . . . 267

**Monsters, Inc.**
The Spooky Sleepover . . . . . . . . . . . 285

# Peter Pan
# The Curse of the Crow

There was nothing Smee hated more than gathering firewood—not even swabbing the decks! But Captain Hook had given him his orders.

The pirate was wandering through the woods when he smelled smoke. Smee chuckled. "If somebody's gathered wood for a bonfire, they've done the work for me!"

In a nearby clearing, Smee found Peter Pan, Tinker Bell, Wendy, John, and Michael gathered around a crackling fire.

"Tell us a scary story, Wendy," Peter Pan said.

A sly smile crossed Wendy's face. "Have you ever heard of the Curse of the Crow?" she asked.

The boys shook their heads.

"Long ago there lived a wise old crow," Wendy began. "Though he was wise, he envied the cleverness of people. Since he could not compete with them, he cursed them instead!

"There were four signs that you had been cursed," Wendy continued. "First there would be bird tracks. Then soot in the soap. And sudden fits of *sneezing*. But worst of all . . ."

"What? What was the worst?" the boys chorused.

"A single black feather would appear on your pillow," Wendy said. "That meant that the crow had *cursed you for life*!"

Just then, a *caw-caw-caw!* rang through the clearing.

Everyone around the bonfire jumped. Smee, who was hiding in the bushes, was so scared that his knees started knocking! He grabbed the nearest pile of twigs and skedaddled all the way back to the *Jolly Roger*.

"Oh, Peter," Wendy said with a laugh. "That was a perfectly timed *caw*, I should say!"

Peter grinned. He had noticed Smee hiding in the bushes and thought to give him a good scare. He was sure the pirate would be shaking for the rest of the night!

"One more story?" Michael asked through a big yawn.

"I'm afraid not, young man," replied Wendy. "It's bedtime for you."

"I'll put out the fire," Peter said.

As he splashed a pail of water onto the bonfire, Peter had an idea. He beckoned to John and Tink. "I know how to teach that Smee a lesson once and for all," he began. "But first we'll need a pine branch, some flowers, and all this soggy soot. . . ."

Meanwhile, Smee had made it back to the *Jolly Roger*. "Captain! Captain!" he cried breathlessly as he ran onto the ship.

"What is it? The Crocodile?" Captain Hook shrieked, jumping.

"No," Smee replied. "It's the Curse of the Crow!" He told the crew Wendy's story, but none of the other pirates were scared.

"Why, there ain't never been a crow in Never Land!" one of the pirates jeered.

"But I heard one," Smee protested.

While Smee was telling the pirates Wendy's story, Peter Pan, Tink, and John snuck onto the *Jolly Roger*.

Peter whispered, "Tink—you're up!"

Tink dipped a pine sprig into the pail of wet soot. Then she flew around the ship, leaving dirty marks that looked just like bird tracks!

When Smee saw the marks, he gasped. "Bird tracks!" he exclaimed. "It's the Curse of the Crow!"

But Captain Hook did not believe in the curse. He just saw a big mess. "You call this shipshape?" he bellowed at his crew. "Swab the decks at once, or you'll walk the plank!"

Smee scrambled to add soap powder to pails of water. "They'll see," he grumbled. "The curse is real!"

"Your turn, John," Peter whispered. "Hurry!"

When Smee's back was turned, John dashed forward and sprinkled more soot into the pails. When the pirates started mopping the deck, they made the mess even worse!

"Oh, *no*," Smee moaned, hiding his eyes. "The crow's curse is happening, just the way Wendy said it would!"

"A cursed ship's not fit to sail," one of the pirates said.

"The only curse you have to worry about is from *me* if you don't clean this up!" Captain Hook growled.

"Now, Tink!" Peter whispered. Tinker Bell grabbed the bunch of flowers and flew high into the air. Then she shook the flowers, sprinkling pollen all over the pirates!

"Nice clean soap, turned black and murky as mud," one of the pirates said anxiously. "Something strange is afoot!"

"Yes," Hook muttered. "I—ah-ah-*achoo*!"

"Sneezing!" gasped Smee. "The next stage of the crow's curse!"

But the pirates were sneezing so loudly that no one could even hear him!

"We—*achoo!*—are—*achoo!*—doomed!" Smee howled between sneezes.

"Now see here," Captain Hook said when his sneezing fit finally died down. "There is *no* Curse of the Crow. This is more like the work of a rascal!"

"What do you mean, Captain?" Smee asked.

"Peter Pan is trying to make fools of us all," Hook explained. "Search the ship and seize that scoundrel!"

"Aye-aye, Captain!" the pirates yelled.

"That's our cue," Peter told the others. "Away we go!"

"Captain! Look!" Smee said in astonishment as he spotted two figures flying past the full moon.

"What did I tell you?" Captain Hook gloated, pushing past Smee and making his way toward his cabin. "I knew there would be an explanation for all this silliness."

"You were right, Captain," Smee said, breathing a sigh of relief. "It was just Peter Pan. After all, it's not like anyone found a crow's feather on his pillow. Now *that* would be really scary. Imagine being cursed . . . for life!"

"You imagine it," Captain Hook retorted. "I'm going to bed."

Captain Hook took his key and unlocked the door to his cabin. "Cursed for life," he said with a chuckle as he lit a candle. "Poppycock!"

Then he saw it: a single dark feather, right on his pillow! Captain Hook's face grew very pale. "P-P-Peter P-P-Pan?" he stammered. But how? The cabin had been locked, and Captain Hook had already seen him fly away!

Perhaps the Curse of the Crow was real, after all!

# Riley's Haunted
# Halloween

**I**t was fall in San Francisco, and everyone was looking forward to Halloween. Everyone, that is, except for Riley. She was finding it hard to get into the Halloween spirit. It would be her first year trick-or-treating without her friends from Minnesota.

One morning at breakfast, Riley told her parents that she would be sitting out Halloween that year. "I'm getting a little old for trick-or-treating, anyway," she said.

Inside Headquarters, Anger was fuming. "Why are we skipping Halloween? We *love* Halloween! Whose bright idea was this, anyway?"

"Take a chill pill," Disgust said. "Riley is twelve now."

"Halloween won't be any fun without our old friends, anyway," Sadness added. "They knew exactly what candy Riley likes. Without them, who will we trade with? We'll be stuck with all the bad candy, and then we'll end up with a cavity and our teeth will fall out and everyone will make fun of us and—"

Joy shook her head, interrupting Sadness before she spiraled out of control. Long Term Memory was packed full of happy Halloween memories. Surely they could have fun in San Francisco, too! "Heads up! Mom and Dad are about to talk," she said.

"Whatever you think is best, Riley," Riley's dad said. "But I bet there are some other new girls who feel the same way. Someone who needs a friend to hang out with. . . ."

"Isn't there another new girl in class? Faye? I bet she'd like to go trick-or-treating, too," Riley's mom added.

"Who's Faye?" Anger asked the other Emotions, confused.

Joy turned to look at Sadness. "We can't let Faye spend Halloween alone! With no friends? And no candy?!"

"That sounds terrible," Sadness said. "She'll probably sit by the window, watching all the other kids have fun without her. She'll think of her friends back home, and then she'll start crying, and then her face will get all puffy and her eyes will get red and no one will want to look at her because all the crying will make her so . . . ugly!"

"Great!" Joy said, cutting off Sadness. "It's agreed: we're doing Halloween! Now we just need to find the perfect moment to get Riley on board. Come on, guys. We can do this!"

21

That week at hockey practice, as Riley laced up her skates, Faye bounded over to her.

"Hey, Riley!" she said. "Um, I was thinking, and . . . do you wanna hang out on Friday? You know, for Halloween?"

"This girl is great!" Joy said, pushing a few buttons on her console. "She just walked right up and did our job for us! Plus, she clearly understands the importance of free candy."

Riley smiled. "Well, I'm not sure if I'm up for trick-or-treating, but would you want to check out the haunted house?"

Faye nodded. "Sure! That sounds like fun!"

Joy spun around. "This is going to be *great*!"

"A haunted house?" Fear said. "It won't be too scary, will it? I mean, the house won't *really* be haunted . . . right?"

"Of course not!" Joy replied. "There will be candy, and spooky lights, and maybe a few parents dressed up as monsters, and candy, and new friends, and candy!"

"Did you say monsters?" Fear asked nervously. "Oh, no. No, no, no. I do *not* like the sound of that!"

"You had me at candy," Anger said. "Let's do this thing!"

The days flew by, and soon it was Halloween. Faye had texted Riley to coordinate their costumes, and Riley's parents had helped her pull together a very convincing pirate costume.

Riley turned to her dad. "Arrrrr, matey! Ye'd best save some candy for me, or I'll have ye walk the plank!"

Riley lifted her sword threateningly.

Riley's dad raised his hands in surrender. "Shiver me timbers! What a fearsome pirate."

"Have fun tonight, Riley," her mom said as Riley ran out the door to meet Faye.

When Riley arrived at the haunted house, she looked around. Faye was waiting outside. She was dressed up as a hook-handed pirate.

"Hey, Riley! Over here!" Faye called, waving the shiny hook she wore over her hand. "Ready to go inside?"

Fear looked at the other Emotions nervously. "Suuuure. What could *possibly* go wrong in a spooky-looking house?" he said in a shaky voice. "You're sure there are no monsters, Joy?"

Joy leaned forward on the console. "In we go!" she cried happily.

Riley took a deep breath and walked up the front steps. A skeleton sat on the porch, holding a sign that read WELCOME BOYS AND GHOULS!

Faye laughed. "So far the scariest thing about this haunted house is the puns."

Joy snorted with laughter. "I *like* this girl!"

Riley laughed, too. Then, stepping forward, she opened the door.

A woman dressed as a vampire greeted the girls. "Velcome to my lair! Please, von't you enjoy a nice treat?"

The woman held out a dark box, and the girls reached in. Inside were what felt like eyeballs!

"Ewwww!" Disgust turned away from the view screen. "Is everyone touching those? That is *not* sanitary!"

"Are—are those *real* eyeballs?" Fear stammered. "Where did they come from? Are they going to take *our* eyeballs?"

Riley was pretty sure the eyeballs were just peeled grapes and the vampire was just the lunch lady from her school. But the girls still giggled as they felt the "eyeballs" squish between their fingers.

Riley and Faye walked toward the next room.

"*ROAR!*" A man in a furry werewolf costume jumped out from behind the door.

"A werewolf! Joy, that's a monster!!!! You guys lied to me! Run for your lives!" Fear screamed. But the other Emotions weren't fooled, and they held him back. It was just a man in a costume.

Riley and Faye laughed, screamed, and ran from the room.

The next room was a giant mirror maze! Faye and Riley practiced their most ferocious pirate poses as they walked through each twist and turn.

"This is cool," Faye said. "I love puzzles."

Joy nudged Sadness. "I'm getting a serious best-friend vibe here."

Riley smiled at Faye in one of the mirrors. "Hey, thanks for inviting me out tonight," Riley said. "I almost skipped Halloween this year, but I'm really glad I came."

"No way! Me too," Faye said. "But then my parents kinda hinted that I should invite you out for Halloween. They were worried you'd spend Halloween at home."

"Hold on," Anger said. "I thought *we* were helping *her*?"

"I think we ended up helping each other," Sadness said sagely.

"Ugh, you're so sappy," Disgust teased Sadness.

"Does it matter?" Joy said, twirling around excitedly. "We just made a new best friend!"

"Wait! My parents told *me* to invite *you* out for Halloween," Riley said. "They thought you might not be doing anything, either."

"Hmmm. I think we've been played!" Faye said. Then she smiled. "I'm having a great time! Maybe parents do know best after all . . . but don't tell my mom I said that!"

Riley grinned at her new friend.

Just then, Faye spotted something on the far wall. "Aha! Here's the way out!"

Together, Riley and Faye left the maze and made their way out of the haunted house.

"Thank goodness we made it out!" Fear cried in relief.

Faye started to say good-bye, but Riley stopped her. "As long as we're dressed up anyway, want to do a little trick-or-treating?"

"Wait, trick-or-treating? You mean, we're not going home yet? We were going to go eat candy! What happened to the happy candy? Who *knows* what kind of monsters are out there?!" Fear sputtered. "Ack! Is that a zombie?"

Joy turned to the other Emotions. "Still feel too old for Halloween?"

Everyone but Fear shook their heads as Sadness said, "Nope. This feels just right."

34

# BIG HERO 6

# Lights Out!

The sun was beginning to set over San Fransokyo. Outside, rain poured down and the wind howled. But inside the Institute of Technology, Hiro and his friends were too busy to notice.

"Okay," Hiro told Fred. "I've upgraded your super suit with a voice-enhancement module. Say something."

"I am Fred, the great and powerful," Fred said in a friendly voice.

Hiro played it back: "I AM FRED, THE GREAT AND POWERFUL!" Now Fred sounded big and threatening!

Across the room, Wasabi tinkered with his powerful new laser sleeves. "Almost there," he murmured to himself. "I just need to turn up the optical amplifier and—"

*BANG!* Wasabi's amplifier smoked and sizzled, and the lights in the lab went out!

"I must have tripped the electrical breaker," Wasabi told his friends over the howling of the wind outside.

Just then, a shape appeared over Wasabi. He jumped up in alarm.

A glowing light began to radiate from the shape. Wasabi breathed a sigh of relief. It was Baymax.

"Your stress level is higher than usual," Baymax said. "Perhaps you would like to consume a piece of chocolate. Chocolate has been found to release endorphins and make people happier."

Fred stepped out of the shadows, and Wasabi jumped again.

"Maybe it wasn't a power surge," Fred said. He held up a comic book. On its cover, a hulking figure soared over a dark city. "It's like what happened in 'Lights Out in the City.' The supervillain Hypervolt wiped out all the power."

Honey looked out the window. "It looks like we're the only building without power," she said.

"What if a bad guy like Hypervolt is after your laser sleeves?" Fred asked. "He could have caused the blackout. Maybe he wants *all* our technology. This could be a dastardly plan to do us in!"

"Well, I *was* featured on that *Physics and You* web series," Wasabi said thoughtfully. "And I *did* talk about the sleeves. Maybe someone saw me and . . . no. That's crazy. Who would want my laser?"

Wasabi looked around. "I'll go to the basement and flip the breaker," he said. But he didn't move.

Wasabi wasn't exactly *scared* of the basement. He just wasn't crazy about it. It was musty and dark, and there were always strange noises. And now, with no power, it would be even creepier than usual. Still, he had almost finished the laser. And he couldn't test it without power!

As Wasabi stood up, Baymax scanned him again. "Your blood
pressure has spiked. Your heart rate has increased. You are anxious,"
Baymax said. "A support system would be helpful."

Hiro could tell that Wasabi was nervous. "We'll all go to the
basement," he said.

"Good idea," Honey agreed.

Wasabi picked up his laser, and he and his friends headed down the stairs to the basement. Shadows swayed and strange shapes lurked against the walls.

"The breaker is in the far corner," Wasabi said.

Wasabi stumbled across the room, the gang on his heels. A long row of high windows lined one wall, with the breaker box underneath. Wasabi stepped closer. Then he gasped. There was something outside the windows!

"Wasabi?" came a strange voice from outside. "Is that you? Wasa-a-a-a-bi?"

"It's Hypervolt! He's after me!" Wasabi screamed.

Just then, a branch crashed into the window. The glass broke and shards flew everywhere. The wind and rain blew in through the opening, and a whoosh of air rushed through the room, slamming the door shut.

"Cover the window, Honey!" Wasabi cried.

Honey grabbed a chem-ball and tossed it at the broken window. The ball exploded, releasing foam that hardened over the opening.

Fred tugged on the door. "It's locked," he said. "The lock must have been triggered when the door slammed shut. We can't get out."

Wasabi's heart began to pound in his chest. He didn't want to be trapped in the dark basement. They had to get the power back on!

Wasabi flipped the breaker, and the lights flickered on. In the corner, he saw a spare optical amplifier. Wasabi breathed a sigh of relief. Quickly, he finished his laser sleeves. Then he used them to cut a large space out of the closed door.

"Way to go, Wasabi!" Fred shouted. "Let's go get that bad guy!"

Together, the gang rushed out of the basement, up the stairs, and outside into the wet, windy night.

From around the corner, the same eerie voice called out. "Wasa-a-a-bi?" A strange hulking figure lurched toward them.

Go Go flung her armored discs at a nearby tree. Each one sliced through a branch. *Thud!* The branches fell around the villain. He was trapped.

"Wasa-a-a-bi?" came the eerie cry once more.

"Let's call the police!" Wasabi said.

"Wait!" Hiro said. "I think the voice is being distorted by the wind." Hiro turned the knob on his voice-enhancement device. "This should take away the wind effect."

As the voice came again, Hiro paused. "That sounds like—"

"Aunt Cass?" Wasabi said.

Hiro rushed forward to clear away the branches.

Aunt Cass held an umbrella over her head, shielding herself from the wind. In the dark, she looked just like a supervillain.

"It was getting late. I figured you guys might be working through dinner, so I brought you something to eat," Aunt Cass explained.

"The lab door was locked, and I would have called, but I forgot my phone at home. I walked around the building and saw Wasabi through a window, but then a branch blew past me and broke the glass. Before I had a chance to let you know I was here, Honey threw something at the opening and covered it up!"

Wasabi jumped up and gave Aunt Cass a hug. "I'm so glad you're not Hypervolt!" he cried.

Just then, the rain stopped, the wind died down, and the stars came out. It was a beautiful night.

"Your stress levels have returned to normal," Baymax told Wasabi as the friends sat down to enjoy the dinner Cass had brought. He watched Wasabi bite into a large wing. "You are no longer afraid. I will make a note of this. Friends and food. They are the perfect cure."

# Winnie the Pooh
## Frankenpooh

**I**t was just the sort of crisp, sparkling autumn afternoon in the Hundred-Acre Wood that filled Piglet's heart with a story bursting to be told. Inside the little pig's house, Tigger leaped out of the overstuffed armchair he was sharing with Rabbit and Gopher. He bounced over to where Piglet was standing, trying to tell his tale.

"Is it a ghost story full o' spookables an' horribibble creatures?"
Tigger asked, clutching himself in a delightful tingle of terror. "Or is it
about a MAD-scientist type?"

"Oh, no!" Piglet protested. "Not mad at all! Quite happy and cheerful,
really." Then, clearing his throat carefully, he began the story. "Once
upon a time . . ."

Tigger listened for a moment and then interrupted Piglet. "Say, it's broad daylight! Even a not-so-scary story has to happen at night, ya know!"

At that, the picture in Piglet's head of a beautiful castle on a bright summer's day suddenly grew dark and stormy.

"Oh, dear," he murmured to himself.

"An'," Tigger continued, "a nice thunderstorm wouldn't hurt the story, either!"

But Piglet wasn't ready to give up on his happy tale. He had a story to tell, and he was going to tell it his way, if no one minded very much.

Piglet thought about what glorious snacks he could whip up in a spotlessly neat and busily buzzing laboratory if he were a pleasant and very cheerful scientist. He wasn't a bit mad. He wasn't even slightly annoyed. Not even at Tigger.

"Mmm," Piglet said as he imagined the scientist holding a dripping sandwich. "Peanut butter and jelly. My favorite. And so very good for you, too!"

"Gasp!" Tigger suddenly interrupted Piglet's thoughts.

"What is it?" Piglet shouted. "What is it?"

"If you're gonna tell a story about a scientist," Tigger continued, "he ought to at least be doin' somethin' terribibble, like creatin' a boogly, boogly MONSTER!"

"A monster?" Piglet answered in a tiny, not-very-hopeful-that-the-story-was-going-to-go-his-way sort of voice.

"Yeah!" Tigger said. "The monster . . . FRANKENPOOH!"

The scientist looked at Frankenpooh with mixed feelings. Pooh? A MONSTER?

"Yeah!" Tigger continued. "That's absitutely perfect. Only he oughta be bigger than that!"

And all at once, Frankenpooh grew bigger! And bigger and bigger, until the very small scientist felt very small indeed!

"Now *that's* what I call a monster," Tigger cried. "Hoo-hoo-hoo!"

"Oh, bother," the giant Frankenpooh sighed.

After much think-think-thinking and scratching of his oversized
ears, the monster Frankenpooh reached a monstrous conclusion.

"I want . . . honey?" he announced in a voice so loud he surprised
himself. And he went looking for a not-so-small smackerel of something
sweet to eat. "Honey!" he announced again, just because he liked the
sound of it.

"And the monster Frankenpooh," Tigger said, "went lookin' high and low for whatever it is monster Frankenpoohs look for."

"Honey," Frankenpooh boomed.

"An' the villagers skedaddled for life and lumber," Tigger continued. "Trembling in your socks, aren't ya? Clinging to the edge of your seats? But there's no stoppin' the gigantical monstrous monstrosity!"

"Everybody was up to their necks in arms," Tigger added dramatically, "because they knew who it was that was responsibibble for the horribibblest monster that was terror-fryin' them."

"Help!" the scientist yelled. "Stop the story! Please! It was an accident! I didn't mean to do it! I just wanted it to be a nice, not-so-scary story."

Piglet opened his eyes to discover himself back on the hearth of his very own fireplace, surrounded by his good friends Tigger, Rabbit, and Gopher.

"But, Piglet," Tigger soothed, "it was nothin' to get so upset about."

"It was just a s-s-silly s-s-story," Gopher whistled.

"Of course, Piglet," Rabbit added gently. "There was no monster. And no one's angry at you."

Piglet looked around in great relief. "No?" he asked in a very small voice.

"No," his friends all assured him at once.

Tigger jumped up to give Piglet a big hug.

After Tigger, Rabbit, and Gopher had settled Piglet in his favorite armchair and given him a cup of his favorite hot chocolate, Rabbit put his arm comfortingly around Piglet's very small shoulder.

"Stories are just stories. You really should learn the difference between what's real and what isn't," Rabbit told him gently. "Shouldn't he, Pooh? POOH?"

"Yes, Piglet," the very large and Frankenpooh-looking bear responded, "you really should. And so should I."

And with that, Frankenpooh settled down to get the story straightened out in his head full of fluff and return to the sort of Pooh Bear his friends loved so dearly.

# Shadows in the Jungle

It was a sunny afternoon in the jungle. The Dawn Patrol was on its afternoon march. Colonel Hathi marched at the front of the line. His son brought up the rear.

"Hup, two, three, four!" the elephants chanted.

As the patrol marched through a row of flowering trees, Colonel Hathi's trunk began to twitch. Then it wiggled. Then . . .

*"Achooooo!"* the colonel sneezed, jerking backward. He bumped into the elephant behind him. That elephant bumped into the next elephant, and *that* elephant into the one behind him. The elephants kept bumping into each other until . . .

*Bam!* The last elephant bumped into Hathi's son. The little elephant tumbled backward into a large hole in the ground.

*Thump!* The baby elephant landed in a heap. He blinked his eyelids and looked around. He was in a cave. Spiders and strange bugs skittered up the walls and across the floor. In front of him, the wind whipped eerily through several dark tunnels.

The elephant didn't know which way to go. He couldn't be sure any of the tunnels would lead him out of the cave, and they all looked so scary!

*"Heeeeeelp!"* he cried.

The elephant's voice echoed throughout the cave. But the Dawn Patrol had already marched on. They didn't hear the little elephant's call for help.

Across the jungle, Shere Khan's ears twitched.

"That sounds like the cry of a helpless animal," the tiger purred in his deep voice. "Music to my ears!"

Shere Khan swiftly made his way toward the sound, his padded feet moving silently across the jungle floor.

Hanging in the nearby trees, three monkeys heard the elephant's call for help, too.

"What's that?" the first monkey asked.

"Let's go see!" the second monkey said.

The monkeys swung from branch to branch, heading toward the noise. But they stopped when they saw Shere Khan.

"Never mind!" the third monkey whispered nervously. "Let's get out of here!"

On the ground below, Mowgli and Baloo were having fun rolling down a hill.

"Hey!" Mowgli called out as the monkeys swung past them. "What's the hurry?"

The monkeys stopped.

"We didn't hear anything!" the first monkey shouted.

"We didn't see anything, either!" the second monkey yelled.

"That's right," said the third monkey. "We definitely did *not* hear a little elephant call out for help or see Shere Khan making his way toward the sound."

Mowgli jumped up. "A little elephant? Hathi's son is in trouble!"

"Which way did you *not* hear a little elephant call for help?" Baloo asked.

The monkeys all pointed over their shoulders, and Baloo and Mowgli ran off to help their friend.

Meanwhile, back in the cave, the light was beginning to fade. The poor baby elephant stared at the tunnels.

"Pop will come for me," he told himself, settling down to wait. "I'm sure the Dawn Patrol will be here any minute to rescue me."

The little elephant shivered. A strange feeling had come over him . . . a feeling that he wasn't alone in the cave anymore.

"Hello?" he called out, his voice shaking. "Is someone there?"

Suddenly, two large yellow eyes appeared in one of the dark tunnels. The little elephant froze with fear as Shere Khan stepped out of the darkness.

"Good afternoon," the tiger said, his eyes fixed intently on the elephant.

76

Mowgli and Baloo heard the elephant's cry. They raced toward the sound as fast as they could. They soon came to a cave in the side of a rocky cliff.

"He must be in there," Mowgli said, starting forward, but Baloo stopped him.

"Look there, little buddy," the bear said.

He pointed to some fresh paw prints leading into the cave. Tiger paw prints!

"We've got to do something," Mowgli said, determined to help his friend. He looked at the cave. He saw the last rays of the setting sun starting to fade.

"Hmmm," Mowgli said, scratching his chin. "I've got an idea, but I'll need your help."

Inside the cave, Shere Khan grinned slyly at the elephant.

"Your father and his elephant patrol are quite fierce," the tiger murmured in his deep, smooth voice. "But you, little one, are another story. You shall make quite a tasty morsel."

The baby elephant gulped. What would his pop do now?

"You won't eat me!" he said, trying to look as brave as he could. "The Dawn Patrol will rescue me!"

Shere Khan shook his head. "They're long gone," he said. "And even if they were here, they do not scare me. Now let us finish this."

The tiger moved forward but then stopped. Shadows had started to flicker on the wall. The little elephant saw Shere Khan's scared face and turned around to look.

"Men!" the elephant cried. "Men with torches!"

Nothing frightened Shere Khan more than Man and his fire. The tiger growled. "Our dinner engagement will have to wait, I'm afraid," he said. And with that, he raced out of the cave.

Hidden from sight, Mowgli and Baloo watched the frightened tiger sprint into the jungle.

When they were sure Shere Khan was gone, Mowgli and Baloo stepped into the cave.

"Are you all right?" Mowgli asked.

"Is that you, Mowgli?" the elephant called. "I'm fine! But how did you find me?"

"We followed the sound of your cry to a cave," Mowgli said. "This tunnel led us right to you."

Mowgli ran to his friend and hugged him. "Don't you worry about Shere Khan," he said. "We got rid of him."

"But where are the men and their torches?" the elephant asked.

Baloo held up some leaves. "Just a little trick of the light!"

The three friends set off through the tunnel and back into the jungle. They came out of the cave just in time to see the Dawn Patrol marching toward them.

"Pop!" the little elephant cried, running up to his father. "I fell into a cave, and Shere Khan almost got me, but Mowgli and Baloo saved me," the little elephant cried.

"Thank you both," Colonel Hathi said. "I am in your debt."

Mowgli grinned. "That's what friends are for!"

# The Ghost-Light Fish

"**H**ave a great day, Nemo!" Marlin the clownfish said as he hugged his son good-bye. Marlin and Dory, a regal blue tang fish, were dropping Nemo off at school.

"All right!" Nemo exclaimed. "I will . . . just as soon as you let go."

Marlin realized he was still hugging his son. "Oh, right!" Marlin said with a chuckle. He let go.

Nemo swam off to join the other students and their teacher, Mr. Ray. "Bye, Dad! Bye, Dory!" the little clownfish called out.

Nemo loved school. So did his friends, Tad the long-nosed butterfly fish, Pearl the octopus, and Sheldon the sea horse. Every day, Mr. Ray took his students exploring all over the reef. That day, he was taking them to a clearing on the ocean floor.

"Okay, explorers," Mr. Ray said when they arrived, "now it's time to do a little searching on your own. Let's see if each of you can find a shell. Then we'll identify them together!"

The youngsters fanned out. Nemo searched in the shadow of some coral. Pearl peeked into a bit of algae. Sheldon dug in the sand.

Tad was the first of Nemo's friends to find something. "Hey, guys!" he cried. "Look at this!"

Nemo, Pearl, and Sheldon swam over to their friend. They crowded
around and stared in wonder at the gleaming white shell Tad held in
his fin.

"Cooooool," Sheldon said.

"It's *so* pretty," Pearl gushed. "Where did you find it?"

Tad pointed to a cave. "In there," he said. "Maybe there are more!"
He darted toward the cave entrance.

"Yeah!" Pearl said, following him. "I want to find one, too."

"Me too!" Sheldon cried. "Are you coming, Nemo?" he asked his friend.

"Nah. You guys go on," Nemo replied. He wanted to find a shell that was different from everybody else's.

Only a few minutes passed before Nemo heard an odd noise. He looked up and saw Sheldon, Tad, and Pearl bolting out of the cave at full speed, screaming loudly.

"What's the matter?" Nemo asked. "Is it a barracuda? An eel?"

Sheldon shook his head. "No, worse!" he said fearfully.

"It's a *g-g-ghost fish*!" Pearl stammered.

Nemo laughed. "Yeah, right," he replied. Then he noticed Tad's fin was empty. "Where's your shell?" he asked.

Tad looked down. "Aw, shucks," he said, disappointed. "I was going to give it to my mom." He peered into the cave. "I must have dropped it in there. But I'm not going back for it. Not with that ghost fish on the loose!"

"Don't worry," Nemo told Tad. "I'll find your shell."

The little clownfish swam bravely into the cave. *See?* he said to himself. *Nothing to be afraid of.*

Suddenly, Nemo froze. On the cave wall next to him was a huge fish-shaped shadow! Nemo took a deep breath. "Uh, excuse me, Mr. Ghost Fish? Or is it Ms. Ghost Fish?" he stammered.

"A ghost fish?" a tiny voice said nervously. "Where? Where? Don't let it get me!"

The ghost fish didn't *sound* very scary. Nemo swam closer.

"Are *you* afraid of ghost fish?" he asked.

"Yeah!" the little voice squeaked. "Who isn't?"

Nemo followed the voice. There, cowering behind a rock, was a little fish, glowing softly with pale orange light. The ghost fish wasn't a ghost fish at all! It was just a glow-in-the-dark fish. Its glow had shined on an oddly shaped piece of coral and made a spooky-looking shadow! Nemo's fear was forgotten.

"Oh, hi!" he called out.

Startled, the glowing fish darted behind another rock. Then, timidly, he peeked out from behind it to study Nemo.

"Don't be afraid," Nemo said. "I'm just a little fish, like you." He smiled. "My name's Nemo. What's yours?"

The fish swam out cautiously. "Eddy," he replied, his eyes still wide. "You mean, there's no ghost fish?"

Nemo chuckled. "I thought *you* were the ghost fish!" He explained the whole funny story.

"By the way," Nemo said, "how do you glow like that?"

Eddy shrugged. "I just do," he replied. "My whole family does."

Nemo thought of someone who would know more about Eddy's glow: Mr. Ray! Nemo invited Eddy to meet his teacher and his friends. Then, swimming out of the cave together, the two little fish laughed about the way they had met.

"You really thought *I* was a ghost fish?" Eddy asked with a giggle.

Outside, Nemo rejoined his friends. "Sorry I didn't find your shell," Nemo said to Tad. "But I did find your ghost fish!" Then Nemo and Eddy told their story. Before long, the ghost fish was forgotten. Instead, everyone wanted to know more about Eddy!

"Can you glow different colors?" Pearl asked.

"How come the water doesn't put out your light?" Tad added.

Nemo wanted to know what made Eddy glow.

"Good question, Nemo," Mr. Ray replied. "See these patches on either side of Eddy's jaw? Inside them are teeny, tiny glow-in-the-dark organisms. When you see Eddy glow, you're really seeing those organisms glowing." Everyone oohed and aahed over Eddy's glow patches.

"If you think that's cool," Eddy said, "you should come meet the rest of my family!"

Eddy led the whole class into the cave to show them his glow-in-the-dark world—including his family. Nemo thought it was one of the most beautiful things he had ever seen. But there was still one thing weighing on his mind.

"Mr. Ray," Nemo whispered to his teacher, "I didn't finish the assignment. I mean, I didn't find a shell."

Mr. Ray laughed. "That's okay, Nemo," he replied. "I'd say you still get an A in exploring for today!"

# Detective Lucky

A blustery wind was blowing outside, but the Dalmatian puppies—all ninety-nine of them—were snug and cozy in their new house. The puppies crowded around Nanny, who was reading them a bedtime story.

Lucky loved bedtime stories. He especially loved ones about detectives! He wished *he* could be a detective.

When Nanny's story was over, Pongo and Perdita tucked the puppies into bed. But Lucky wasn't tired—not even a little bit! He couldn't stop thinking about all the mysteries he would solve if he were a detective.

One by one, the other puppies drifted off to sleep. Soon Lucky was the only one still awake. Suddenly, his ears twitched.

*Creak, squeak, BANG!*

What was that strange sound? Lucky bolted upright. Maybe this was it—the mystery he had wished for. Maybe the sound was a clue!

Lucky carefully climbed out of bed. His parents were in the living room with Roger and Anita. No one would notice if Lucky slipped through the doggie door. He could go outside, find some clues, crack the case, and be back before anyone even knew that he'd left!

Lucky scampered outside. He looked around. He had never been outside alone at night. The wind had died down, but it was very dark. All around him, Lucky saw strange shadowy shapes.

Lucky thought about going back inside. But he knew that a true detective would solve his case no matter what. If he wanted to be a detective, he'd have to go on, dark or no dark.

Lucky sniffed the air. An unfamiliar smell made his nose twitch. Maybe it was another clue!

Lucky pressed his nose down to the dirt and sniffed again. There it was—the same smell! His tail wagged as he followed the scent into the woods.

*This is exactly what a real detective would do!* Lucky thought eagerly as he tracked the smell to a hollow log. Lucky poked his head into the log to see what was inside—and found two spooky eyes staring back at him!

Lucky yelped in surprise. He backed out of the log as quickly as he could—and ran right into a tree. *Thunk!*

Strange noises filled the air, and Lucky felt something brush by his head.

*Hoo-hoo-hoo-hoo!*

*Flap-flap-flap-whooooooosh!*

Lucky was surrounded by spooky sounds, and he didn't know what was making any of them. And to make matters worse, he'd been so busy tracking the smell that he hadn't noticed how far he'd roamed. He had no idea where he was or how to get home!

There was only one thing to do. Run!

Lucky raced through the forest, ducking under branches and leaping over rocks. When the trees began to thin, he charged forward, running faster and faster until—*wham!* He knocked right into someone!

In a flurry of fur and tails and hisses and growls, Lucky and the stranger tumbled over and over and over. Then a familiar voice said, "Lucky? Is that you?"

It was Sergeant Tibs, the cat who'd helped rescue Lucky and his

siblings from Cruella De Vil!

"Sergeant Tibs!" Lucky cried
in relief. "Help! I'm lost and I don't
know how to get home!"

Sergeant Tibs knew just
what to do. He led Lucky to
an old barn, where the two
filled the Colonel in on Lucky's situation.

"No question about it, we've got to get this pup back to the Dalmatian

Plantation," the Colonel announced. "But it's too late for the Twilight

Bark, I'm afraid."

Lucky's heart sank. "You mean I have to stay here all night?" he

asked.

"No need for that," the Colonel said kindly. "This calls for the

Midnight Bark!"

The Colonel lumbered over to the door and howled into the night. Lucky waited anxiously for a response. At last, it came!

*Bark! Bark! Bark!*
*Yip! Yip-yip! Yip, yip, yip!*
*Arf, arf, arooooo!*

The barks echoed across the countryside to the Dalmatian Plantation, where a sleepy Pongo opened his eyes.

"It's a lost pup," he whispered to Perdita. "I'll go help."

"Follow the barks. They'll lead you home again," the Colonel told Lucky. "Good luck, lad!"

"Thank you," Lucky told the Colonel and Sergeant Tibs. Then, listening closely, he ran into the night. The Colonel was right. Following the sound of the barks, Lucky soon realized that he was on the path home. And now that he was less scared, Lucky was able to solve all the mysteries that he'd stumbled upon—even the creaky old gate that had started it all.

Back at the Dalmatian Plantation, Pongo was shocked to see Lucky bound up to him. "The Midnight Bark was for *you*?" he asked.

"Dad! Dad! I solved a mystery!" Lucky exclaimed. "Just like a real detective!"

"Tell me all about it in the morning," Pongo whispered as he led Lucky back to bed. "And no more mysteries tonight!"

Lucky agreed and snuggled up next to his siblings, ready to fall asleep after his big adventure. Suddenly, his ears twitched.

*Cro-a-a-a-a-k-squeak!*

What was that strange sound?

Maybe it was a clue!

# Beauty and the Beast

# Belle's Mysterious Message

**N**ight had fallen on the Beast's castle, but Belle could not sleep. Her new home still felt strange and lonely, and she could not stop thinking about her father. She hoped he had made it safely back to the village.

"Lumiere," Belle said, "do you think I could read for a little while? Perhaps it would help me fall asleep."

"But of course, mademoiselle!" the candelabrum replied.

Smiling, Belle picked up Lumiere, and the two headed to the castle's large library. Soon Belle had chosen a tall stack of books. She began to make her way across the polished floor when . . . *Crash!* Books went flying in every direction.

Belle knelt down to retrieve a book that had slid underneath the bookshelf. "I think there's something else under here," she said, pulling out a dusty old book. "Look! This has definitely been under there for quite a long time."

Belle added the book to her pile and carefully headed upstairs. The hallway was dark and spooky. But with the cheerful Lumiere as her guide, Belle was soon back in her room.

Settling into bed, Belle picked up the mysterious book and began to read.

The story was about
a knight and a beautiful
princess whose kingdom
was being terrorized by a
dragon. Bravely, the knight
rode out to defeat the evil
dragon. Belle eagerly turned
the pages. But when she
reached the end of the book,
she found a surprise.

"The last chapter is
missing!" she cried, showing
Lumiere. "Perhaps the pages
fell out under the bookshelf."

"We will have to look
tomorrow," Lumiere replied.

The next morning, when Cogsworth came to fetch Belle for breakfast, she asked him about the book.

"When the master was a boy, his tutor made him read this book," Cogsworth said with a smile. "But, alas, the master was a little short-tempered. He threw the book and pages fell out."

As Cogsworth flipped fondly through the pages of the book, a small slip of paper fell out.

"A note!" Belle exclaimed.

Belle opened the note. "'Young Master,'" she read. "'Destroying books in fits of rage will not be tolerated. If you want the final chapter back, you must find it! This is your first clue. Monsieur LeBeau.'"

Belle flipped the note over.

"'To find this clue, you'll be hard put. On a dark gray night, it's underfoot.'"

Cogsworth started to pace back and forth. "We need to think of something that would be under your feet on a dark night," he said. "Any suggestions?"

The three friends looked at each other. Finding the last chapter of the book wasn't going to be easy!

That afternoon, Belle and her new friends searched the castle from top to bottom. As they entered the hall of armor, Belle sighed. "Will we ever find something that's underfoot on a dark gray night?"

Suddenly, they heard a tiny voice echo through the long hallway. "Hey, these knights look pretty gray!"

Startled by the sudden noise, Cogsworth jumped into Lumiere's arms.

"Chip! You scared us." Belle laughed. "But you might be right. Maybe the clue was talking about a gray *knight*."

Belle looked beneath one of the feet of a suit of armor. Sure enough, there was another clue!

"'It's big. It's grand. It's for all to see. You'll find it under number seventy-three,'" Belle read.

"Grand? Why, that must be the grand piano," Cogsworth said.

The friends hurried to the music room, but there was nothing hidden inside the piano.

Cogsworth paced back and forth, thinking hard. "This is more difficult than I thought," he said

"Stop pacing, Cogsworth!" Lumiere cried. "You are making me nervous!"

Cogsworth glared at the candelabrum. "What else is 'grand' around here?" he asked.

*Everything,* Belle thought. *The grand staircase alone is bigger than . . .*

"That's it!" she shouted, running out of the room.

Belle's friends followed her to the grand staircase.

"Under number seventy-three," Cogsworth said thoughtfully.

The friends counted the steps together. Finally, under the seventy-third step, they found clue number three!

"'The next clue? It's found within two brothers who were very grim.'"

Belle thought hard. The clue sounded so familiar to her. *Two brothers who were very grim . . .*

"*The Brothers Grimm!*" she exclaimed.

Cogsworth and Lumiere looked at Belle in confusion.

"The Brothers Grimm were two brothers who collected and wrote fairy tales," she explained. "To the library!"

"Where is the fairy-tale section?" Chip asked as they entered the library.

"It's up there, on the highest shelf," Belle said, pointing.

Everyone watched in disbelief as Belle began to climb.

"Please, be careful," Cogsworth said nervously.

At the very top of the bookshelf, Belle found the Brothers Grimm book. She tucked it into her apron and descended the ladder. Back on solid ground, Belle held the book upside down and shook it. "Nothing," she said sadly.

"The clue is right here," Chip said, pointing to a piece of paper. "It must have fallen out while you were climbing down!"

Belle smiled and picked up the paper. "'Final clue, you're almost home. You'll find it underneath the gnome,'" she read.

"What's a gnome?" Chip asked.

"Gnomes are tiny creatures with long white beards and pointy hats," Belle explained.

"Any ideas, Cogsworth?" Lumiere asked.

"That does sound kind of familiar," Cogsworth replied. "I remember the young master talking about a gnome. Or was it an elf?" He sighed. It was so long before, it was very hard to remember.

Belle turned to the others. "We need to ask the Beast," she said.

Belle marched upstairs to the Beast's study. She knocked loudly, but there was no answer. Opening the door, she peered inside. The Beast turned to her angrily.

"So you don't show up for breakfast and then you trespass?" he growled.

"I'm sorry," Belle said. "But . . . "

The Beast was not in the mood to listen. Throwing open his door, he raced down the stairs past the others.

"But we found a note from Monsieur LeBeau!" Belle called after him. "We need your help!"

Belle's friends shuffled into the room to comfort her.

"I know I came in uninvited," she said, "but he didn't need to be such a . . . beast!"

"I know," a deep voice said. It was the Beast! "I was very rude, and I apologize. Did I hear you say something about my old tutor?"

Belle handed the book to the Beast.

"My book!" he exclaimed.

"Monsieur LeBeau left you a series of clues that lead to the missing chapter!" Belle told him.

"He knew I didn't like to study," the Beast said. "I used to hide in the garden next to a gnome-shaped rock."

"Did you say gnome?" Belle asked eagerly.

The Beast led everyone outside to the garden.

"There he is!" the Beast said, pointing to a rock that resembled a gnome with a pointy hat. Belle watched as the Beast began digging in the earth. A few moments later, he pulled a rusted tin box from the ground. Inside was the missing chapter and a note:

"'Young Master: Good work! We may have our differences, but I can see in you the fine man you will become. Your humble tutor, Monsieur LeBeau.'"

The Beast handed the chapter to Belle. "Would you?" he asked shyly.

Belle smiled and took the pages. And as her friends gathered around her, she began to read the last chapter of the book.

Looking at Belle, the Beast sighed happily. He had been waiting many years to find out how the story ended. Perhaps, he thought, this would be just the first of many happy endings.

# Toy Story of Terror!

**I**t was a dark and spooky night. A woman was being chased through a cemetery by a vampire. The vampire was getting closer . . . and closer. Suddenly, someone screamed.

"Run, Betsy, Run!" Rex called out.

Bonnie and her family were in the car, on their way to a family vacation. Bonnie's toys were in the trunk of the car, watching a scary movie.

"Bor-ing," Mr. Potato Head grumbled.

"Patience," Mr. Pricklepants advised. "All great horror films start slowly."

Mr. Pricklepants was an expert on scary movies. In fact, he considered himself an expert on all movies. And plays. And books . . .

Inside the car, Bonnie rubbed her eyes. "Are we there yet?" she asked with a yawn.

"Not for a few more hours," her mom replied. "You can go back to sleep."

*Ka-thump!* Just then, the car hit a pothole and blew a tire.

The toys went flying. Jessie fell into a toolbox and the lid slammed shut. "Help!" she screamed.

Woody and Buzz Lightyear jumped into action. The two forced open the box and helped Jessie climb out.

Jessie was frightened. "I couldn't . . . I couldn't find a way out," she said, gasping.

"What's the matter with Jessie?" Trixie whispered.

"She was abandoned in a box for years," Mr. Potato Head explained.

Outside, thunder boomed and lightning flashed. The storm was getting worse.

Bonnie's mom pulled over at a roadside motel. The family would be staying there until the tire on their car was fixed. Bonnie reached into the trunk and grabbed her toys.

"A roadside motel is one of the most common locales for a horror film," Mr. Pricklepants pointed out when they reached their room.

Mr. Potato Head decided to go look around.

"I wouldn't go out there if I were you," Mr. Pricklepants warned. "The first to leave usually gets it."

Mr. Potato Head scoffed. He wasn't worried.

137

The toys went after Mr. Potato Head, but he had vanished!

"Maybe this place is haunted," Mr. Pricklepants whispered.

The toys split up to look for Mr. Potato Head. Suddenly, Rex screamed!

"Ewww! I stepped in something," he said, trying to wipe a mysterious goo off his foot.

As Buzz looked around, he realized that Mr. Potato Head had stepped in the same stuff. He had left a trail of footprints!

Trixie followed the tracks to an air vent. As she looked down, she fell in and disappeared!

"Once the heroes enter, there's no turning back," Mr. Pricklepants noted.

The toys followed Trixie into
the vent, Buzz's glow-in-the-dark
features lighting the way.

"What happens now?" Rex
asked Mr. Pricklepants.

"This would be the part where
the characters get separated
and then picked off one by one,"
answered the hedgehog.

Seconds later, something snatched Mr. Pricklepants! Then
it snatched Rex! Woody, Jessie, and Buzz looked at each other and ran!

Just then, something slowly crept out of the darkness toward them.
It was Mr. Potato Head's arm!

"It's trying to tell us something," Buzz said.

"It's the number one," Woody said.

"I think, maybe, it's pointing up," Jessie said.

Above the toys was a vent. The trio followed it to a bathroom.

As Jessie looked around, something snatched Woody and Buzz! Then something pulled Jessie under the sink. It was Combat Carl, a soldier toy with a missing hand. "This place isn't safe for toys," he warned her.

The pair heard a noise. "We're trapped!" Jessie cried.

"Combat Carl never gives up," the soldier toy said. "Combat Carl finds a way."

The toys tried to run, but something snatched Combat Carl. Jessie was on her own.

The cowgirl hid in the bathtub. Seconds later, she heard a loud *RRRIPP!* Claws slashed at the shower curtain! As Jessie backed up, an iguana appeared. It had Mr. Potato Head's arm in its mouth!

Jessie prepared for the worst, but the iguana was actually friendly. It swallowed the arm in one gulp and then gave Jessie a big lick. Grabbing her gently in its mouth, the iguana carried the cowgirl to a room behind the motel's lobby. He set her in a basket and rang a bell. *Ding!*

"Excellent find, Mr. Jones," the manager said, coming into the back room. He had trained his pet iguana to steal toys from motel guests so he could sell them on the Internet.

The manager posted Jessie's picture on a website and put her in a glass cabinet. The cowgirl's friends were there, too— even Combat Carl and his friend Combat Carl Junior.

A few minutes later, the manager returned. He checked his computer. He had sold Woody!

Reaching into the cabinet, he grabbed the cowboy and packed him in a box. A delivery truck would be arriving soon to pick up the package.

"Woody!" Jessie whispered sadly.

"What started out as a classic horror film has turned into something more of a tragedy," Mr. Pricklepants observed.

A few minutes later, the manager sold Jessie, too. He had just taken her out when the mechanic arrived to fix Bonnie's car. The manager put Jessie down and went to speak with the mechanic.

Jessie tried to unlock the cabinet, but she couldn't reach the latch. Even worse, the delivery truck had arrived. The driver came into the back room and took the package with Woody inside!

Jessie didn't know what to do, but Combat Carl had a plan.

"Listen," he said, "in a few minutes, the delivery lady is going to come through that door and take the other boxes, and you're going to be in one of them."

Jessie panicked. "I can't get in a box!" she said.

"Jessie!" the soldier shouted. "When Combat Carl gets stuck in a jam, he says to himself, 'Combat Carl never gives up. Combat Carl finds a way.' Now say it!" he ordered.

Jessie tried. "Combat Carl never gives up. Combat Carl—"

"You're not Combat Carl!" he shouted at her.

"Oh. Jessie never gives up. Jessie finds a way!" the cowgirl repeated, finally understanding.

Jessie snuck into the empty lobby. Opening one of the boxes the manager had packed, she freed a robot toy. Bravely, Jessie crawled into the box in the robot's place. If she could get on the delivery truck, she could free Woody.

The plan was working—until the delivery lady taped the box shut and threw it in the truck!

Jessie began to panic. Then she remembered Combat Carl's words. "Jessie never gives up. Jessie finds a way," she told herself.

Feeling around, the cowgirl found a paper clip. She used it to slit the tape and crawled out of the box. Then Jessie found Woody. The two returned to the back room to free their friends!

Suddenly, Jessie heard Bonnie's voice coming from the lobby. The car was fixed. Bonnie's family was getting ready to leave!

The cowgirl raced toward the curtain that separated the back room from the lobby. She was almost there when Mr. Jones caught her. Jessie kicked the iguana, and it spit something out.

"My hand!" Combat Carl shouted from inside the cabinet.

Mr. Potato Head's arm was also inside the iguana's mouth. Jessie grabbed the arm and used it to pull the curtain open.

At that moment, Bonnie looked through the curtain and saw the cabinet. "My toys!" she cried, running into the back room.

"Are those my daughter's toys?" Bonnie's mom asked the nervous motel manager.

Meanwhile, Mr. Jones put Jessie in a basket on the floor and rang the bell.

Looking down, Bonnie saw the cowgirl. "Jessie!" the little girl shouted, pointing at her doll.

Later, back in the trunk of Bonnie's car, the toys celebrated. "You did it, Jessie. You saved us all," Buzz said.

"Jessie didn't give up. Jessie found a way," the cowgirl said.

Mr. Potato Head looked fondly at his arm. "We ain't never gonna get separated again," he said.

*Ka-thump!* Just then, the car hit a bump. Mr. Potato Head's parts scattered around the trunk. "Aw, nuts," he said.

Everyone laughed, and that, Mr. Pricklepants noted, was a sure sign the story had reached its end.

# Disney
# ALICE
## in
## WONDERLAND
# Queen of Frights

"**W**here are we going again?" Alice asked the Mad Hatter as they dashed through Wonderland together.

"Where isn't the right question," the Mad Hatter said.

"Well then, what *is* the right question?" Alice asked, confused.

"Not what. Why?" the Mad Hatter replied. "*What* we are doing is having fun. You should ask me *why* we are going."

Alice shook her head. Wonderland logic was a bit confusing, but she was finally getting the hang of it. "Very well," she said. "*Why* are we going?"

"I don't know why," the Mad Hatter answered. "I just know that we are in a hurry!"

The Mad Hatter rushed along, and a curious Alice followed behind. Overhead, the sky grew dark and fat raindrops began to fall.

The Mad Hatter plucked a flower and handed it to her. "A little rain never hurt anyone. Here, use this!"

Nearby, at the castle, the
Queen of Hearts was feeling
quite cranky. She had not
slept well the night before
and was in need of a good,
long nap.

"If anyone disturbs me,
I will have their head!"
she barked at the guards
as she stomped into her royal
chamber.

Spotting the rain streaming in
through her open window, the Queen frowned.

"Nasty rain," she muttered, closing the shutters tight. Then she took
off her crown, placed it gently on the table beside her, and climbed into
bed.

In no time at all, the Queen of Hearts was sound asleep. But the Queen was not a quiet sleeper, and she was soon snoring so loudly that she woke herself up! When she opened her eyes, she saw that the table beside her was empty.

"My crown!" she cried, jumping up out of bed.

The Queen of Hearts looked around frantically. Finally, she spotted the crown on the other side of the room!

"This is some kind of trick!" the Queen said. Then she raised her voice so that everyone could hear her. "Whoever is trying to trick me will LOSE THEIR HEAD!"

The Queen climbed back into bed and closed her eyes. But before she could even start snoring, a strange sound filled the room.

*Creeeeeeak . . . creeeeeeak . . . creeeeeak . . .*

"What *is* that racket?" she cried, sitting up.

Then she saw her rocking chair swaying back and forth . . . back and forth . . .

"*Hmph!* It must be a breeze," the Queen told herself. But the window and the shutters were shut tight—just as she had left them. Something else was moving the chair!

"Who's there?" the Queen yelled. She tried to sound threatening, but her voice was beginning to shake. She stomped across the room and stopped the rocking chair from rocking. Then she climbed back into bed and tried to go back to sleep.

The Queen of Hearts closed her eyes. She had just started to snore when a new noise woke her up!

*Squeeeak . . . squeeeeak . . . squeeeeak . . .*

The Queen bolted up in bed. She saw the doors to her wardrobe swinging wide open. The hinges were making an eerie squeaking sound.

"Wh-whoever is t-t-trying to t-t-trick me will l-l-lose th-th-their h-h-head," the Queen stuttered in a frightened whisper. She ran up and closed the wardrobe doors. Then she turned to go back to bed.

*Creeeeeak . . . creeeeak . . . creeeeak . . .*

The Queen spun around. Something had come out of the wardrobe! It had legs, but no feet. It had arms, but no hands. And worst of all, it had no head!

*"Aaaaaaaaaaah!"* the Queen of Hearts screamed. "A GHOST!"

Alice and the Mad Hatter had just arrived outside the castle when they heard the Queen's screams.

"Oh my. Is this where we are?" the Mad Hatter said. "Here is *not* a good where. We should go!"

As Alice turned to follow the Mad Hatter, she spotted something on the ground. "I think I know *why* we are doing what we are doing," she said. "We need to go inside that castle."

A few moments later, Alice and the Mad Hatter burst into the Queen's chamber.

"Ghost! Ghost!" the Queen of Hearts yelled. She was as white as a sheet, and trembling from head to toe.

Alice marched up to the ghost and pulled off its shirt. It was the March Hare! The little Dormouse peeked out of the front pocket of the March Hare's jacket.

"I remember now!" the Mad Hatter cried. "We were playing hide-and-seek!"

"We were looking for a place to hide," the March Hare said. "But nowhere seemed to work. The crown was too small, the chair was too creaky, and the wardrobe was too stuffy!"

The Queen of Hearts turned a deep shade of red. "OFF WITH YOUR HEADS!" she screamed.

The Mad Hatter knew when it was time to go. He tapped the March Hare on the shoulder. "You're It!" he cried. Then he ran off.

Alice followed him. The palace guards chased after her.

"Off with their heads!" the Queen of Hearts screamed again.

Outside, the rain had stopped. But luckily, the ground was still muddy. The guards slipped and slid, giving Alice and her friends a chance to get away.

Back in the Mad Hatter's garden, Alice and her friends enjoyed a nice cup of tea.

"That was fun!" the Mad Hatter exclaimed.

The March Hare agreed. "Let's play another game," he said.

"What do you say, Alice?" the Mad Hatter asked.

"I think I've had enough games for one day," Alice replied. "I'm quite fond of my head, and I'd like to keep it!"

# Mickey's Slumber Party

"**Pluto, I have a** wonderful idea!" Mickey Mouse said one rainy afternoon. "Let's invite our friends over for a slumber party tonight!"

Pluto barked happily. They had been stuck inside all day, and he was ready for some excitement.

While Mickey called his friends, Pluto dragged sleeping bags and pillows into the living room. Soon he and Mickey were ready for the party.

Daisy, Minnie, and Donald arrived just as the rain began to come down harder.

"I brought hot cocoa!" Minnie said, pulling out a thermos. "And mini-marshmallows!"

"Just the thing for a rainy day like this," Mickey said, guiding his friends to the warm fireplace. He poured a mug for each of them.

Daisy looked around. "Where's Goofy?" she asked.

Mickey frowned. "He couldn't make it," he said.

Outside, the wind was blowing hard enough to make the trees sway. Storm clouds covered the moon. Bolts of lightning zapped through the darkness, illuminating the raindrops splashing down.

"You know what it's the perfect weather for?" Mickey asked. "Scary stories! And I know just the one to tell."

As the friends got comfortable, Mickey turned off the lights and began his story.

"Not long ago, in a village not far from here, there lived a young man who wanted to be a magician. The villagers laughed and told him that magic wasn't real. But he worked hard, and finally he was able to make things disappear!

"The villagers still did not believe in his magic. When he made things vanish in front of them, they accused him of tricking them. The magician was angry that no one believed him, and so he began to make the villagers disappear, one by one.

"Soon everyone in the village had disappeared. But the magician had grown to enjoy making people vanish. So now he wanders the land, looking for more victims. He points his long arms at anyone he sees and—"

*BOOM!* A huge crash of thunder shook Mickey's house, and the front door flew open. A great gust of wind blew out the fire, and everyone screamed.

"It's okay!" Mickey reassured them as he got up to close the door. "It's just the wind!" He tried to flick on a light, but nothing happened. "The storm must have knocked out the power. I'll go find some flashlights."

Minnie giggled. "I was so caught up in Mickey's story, I thought it was the magician coming through the door!"

174

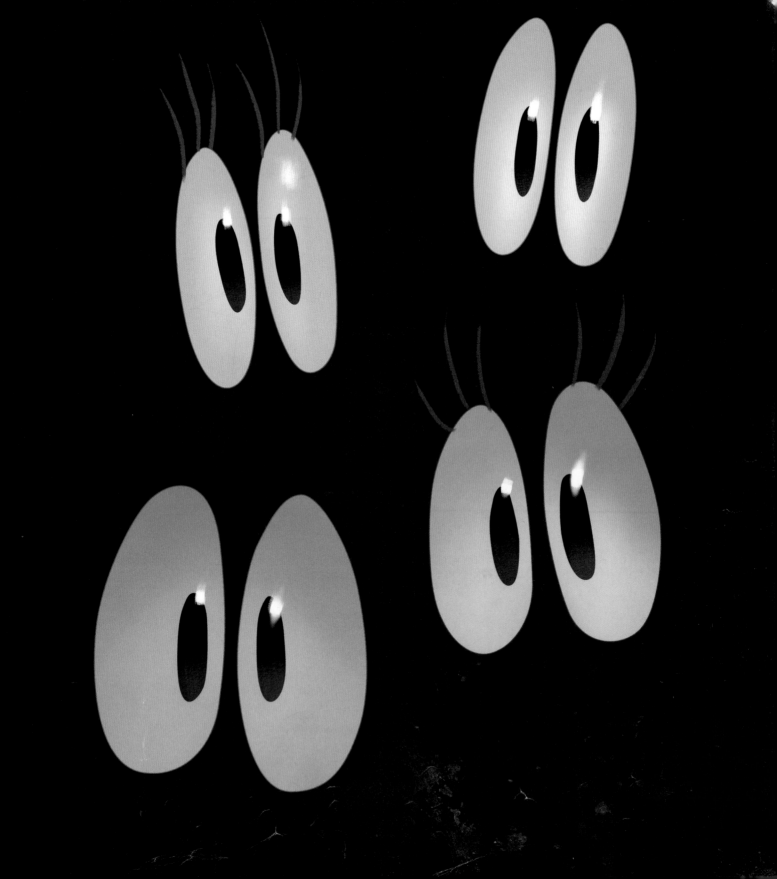

Soon Mickey came back with a candle. "This is the only thing I could find," he said. "I don't know where all the flashlights could be."

"Mickey, where's Pluto?" Daisy asked as the candle lit up their circle. The four friends looked around, but Pluto was gone.

"Pluto?" they called. There was no answer.

The friends got up and began to look around. Donald even opened the front door and shouted into the rain. "Pluto!"

"Maybe it really was the evil magician who caused the lights to go out!" Daisy whispered. "And he made Pluto vanish!"

"Don't be silly, Daisy," said Minnie, looking around nervously. "That was just a story Mickey made up to scare us. Right, Mickey?"

Just then, the door to the basement creaked open. Mickey, Donald, Daisy, and Minnie jumped and turned in time to see a floating white shape entering the room.

"It's a ghost!" Donald cried.

"He's going to get us!" Daisy gasped, hugging Minnie.

The white sheet slipped away to reveal a familiar face.

"It's only Pluto!" Mickey said happily, going to help his friend. Pluto had gone to the basement to find flashlights. His mouth was full of them.

Daisy hugged Pluto as he and Mickey passed out the flashlights. "I'm so glad you're safe!" she said. "We've been scaring ourselves with silly things while you were gone. We thought the evil magician made you disappear!"

"I think I've had enough scary stories for one night!" Mickey said. "What should we do now?"

"I know," Minnie said. "Since we have all these flashlights, why don't we make shadow puppets?"

"That sounds like fun!" Donald said. "How do you make them?"

"I'll show you," Minnie replied.

Minnie helped Donald move his hands into a particular shape. Then Mickey held up the flashlight behind them, and a shadow turtle appeared on the wall!

"Wow!" Donald exclaimed. He moved his fingers, and the turtle's head bobbed up and down.

"Daisy, hold your hands like this," Minnie said. When Pluto raised his flashlight behind them, a rabbit appeared next to the turtle. Daisy wiggled her fingers, and the rabbit's ears moved.

"Now we can act out the story of the tortoise and the hare!" Minnie said with a smile.

As Minnie began to tell the story, Donald and Daisy moved their shadow puppets on the wall. Just then a bright flash of lightning lit up the whole living room, replacing the shadow puppets with the shadow of a huge long-armed figure standing by the front door.

"It's the evil magician!" Donald shouted.

Mickey and Pluto swung their flashlights around to see the frightening figure.

"Gawrsh," Goofy said as he stepped through the door, taking off his wet poncho. "I didn't mean to scare ya. But it turns out I can join you for the slumber party after all! Say, who turned off the lights?"

"Mickey told us a story about an evil magician who makes people disappear," Minnie said. "We thought you were him."

"That sounds scary," Goofy said. "I know another scary story if you want to hear it."

"No!" the friends all shouted together.

Goofy held up his guitar. "How about a few songs instead?" he asked.

Minnie nodded. "I think a sing-along is much safer than telling stories," she said. Mickey lit the fire again, and as the wind and thunder calmed outside, the friends sang together.

Soon everyone was yawning. The friends snuggled up in their sleeping bags.

"Good night, everyone," Mickey said.

And with the sound of soft rain filling the room, they all fell asleep.

# BRAVE
# Merida's Wild Ride

It was a soggy, stormy afternoon. Merida sat in the stables reading from an old book of Highland tales. She and her horse, Angus, wanted to go for a ride—if only the weather would clear up.

"Look at this picture of a brownie," Merida said. "The book says they're little goblins who cause mischief unless you keep them well fed. Sounds like my brothers. . . ."

Angus snorted, shaking his head. It was clear that he wanted nothing to do with magical creatures, especially after their last encounter.

Even though Merida had been able to transform her mum back from a bear to a human, Merida had learned that magic was not to be taken lightly.

189

Merida read on until the raindrops slowed and the clouds began to scatter.

"Come, lad," said Merida to Angus. "The sun's breaking through. Let's go for a ride."

They galloped across the bridge and down the hill. But just as they reached the woods, Merida saw a flash of gray dart through the trees. "What was that?" she cried.

Angus didn't want to follow it—whatever it was.

"Don't be a ninny," Merida chided him. "I'm sure it's not a bear." But what was it? Merida guided Angus into the woods, keeping her eyes open for another glimpse of the creature.

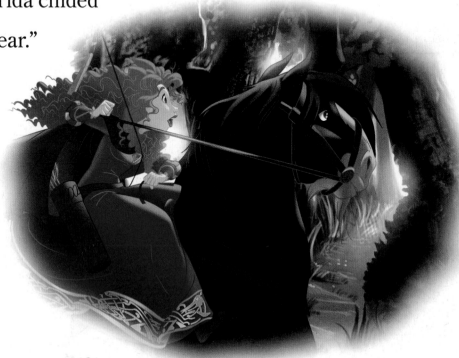

As they rode, Merida kept catching flashes of the animal. She urged Angus to go faster until they broke through the trees and into a clearing. There stood a magnificent gray horse. Its coat shimmered. Its mane was like fine silk.

Breathless with excitement, Merida whispered to Angus, "He's beautiful."

Merida dismounted and approached the horse with a gentle smile. "Come here. I won't hurt you."

Suddenly, Angus blocked Merida's path.

"Angus," she called, "don't be jealous, lad! This horse must be lost. We need to help him—make sure he's safe."

Merida cooed to the gray horse, and it responded with a soft whinny.

"See, Angus? He's friendly." Merida stroked the new horse's nose playfully. "Now I'll ride him back to the castle, and you follow close behind. Okay, Angus?"

Merida had a spare bridle in Angus's pack, but she decided not to use it. She didn't want to spook the horse with unfamiliar reins. Instead, Merida decided she could guide him with her hands wrapped in his mane.

Angus gave a resigned snort as Merida swung up onto the gray horse's back. But as soon as she mounted him, the horse reared wildly.

Merida tried to calm the horse, but he started running. Faster and faster, the strange horse galloped until the field was far behind them. Soon the trees began to thin, and Merida gasped in horror. They were racing toward the edge of a cliff!

Merida tried everything she could to get the horse to stop, but nothing worked! She realized her only choice was to leap from the horse's back.

But when she moved to jump, her hands were stuck to the horse's mane. His hair wasn't sticky or knotted, yet Merida could not free her hands. It was as if they were held there by magic.

Merida tried to slide off the side of the horse, but nothing could free her hands from his mane. She thought she was out of options. Then, suddenly, the runaway horse brushed against the trunk of a tree. Trapped rainwater fell down around  Merida. Effortlessly, one of her hands came loose.

But Merida's other hand was still stuck. Merida did the only thing she could think of.

"Angus!" she cried. "Help!" Merida could only hope that her friend had heard her cry.

Merida looked up at the sound of a whinny. Angus galloped up next to them—and he was carrying the spare bridle in his mouth! He must have pulled it from his pack to help Merida.

Angus tossed it through the air just as they were nearing the cliff's edge. Merida caught it with her free hand and slipped it over the horse's head. As soon as the horse was bridled, Merida's trapped hand came free. With the reins, she turned the horse away from the steep drop-off.

Now that the horse had calmed down, Merida guided him to a safe path beside the sea. As they reached the shore, the horse finally slowed to a stop. Grateful, Merida jumped off.

The stallion stood quietly. Merida looked in his eyes for an answer about what had caused the wild ride. It was clear to her that this was no ordinary horse. It must be a creature of magic.

Merida removed the bridle and whispered quietly, "What are you?"

But the horse did not reply. He simply moved his head softly, as if he was nodding, before galloping down the misty shoreline and into the water.

Merida frowned as she watched him. As the horse raced deeper into the sea, he seemed to disappear into fog.

Merida mounted Angus and returned home. She was glad that the strange horse had not harmed her, but she wanted an explanation for her wild ride.

Back at the stable, Merida flipped through the book of Highland legends, looking for answers, until she saw a picture of a very familiar horse.

"Look!" She showed the book to Angus. "It's a kelpie. The book says, 'Once a bridle is put on a kelpie, the water horse will do your bidding.'"

Angus snorted in disbelief.

"Don't worry, lad," Merida said. "I won't be riding another one any time soon. You're the only horse for me."

Angus nuzzled his head against Merida's hand as if to reply that she was the only girl for him.

# THE LION KING

# A Dark and Scar-y Night

**S**car sighed, watching the afternoon sun sink lower in the sky. Life just wasn't fair. *He* should be ruling over the Pride Lands, not his brother, Mufasa.

"Oh, Scar!" someone called in a singsong. It was Mufasa's steward, Zazu. "I bring an important announcement from the king!"

"And what, pray tell, does Mufasa want?" Scar asked the bird, lazily picking something out of his claws.

"*King* Mufasa," Zazu said, correcting him, "has decided it is time to prepare Simba for his future reign. He would like everyone to tell him tales of kings past this evening—a family story time, as it were."

Scar tensed. If there was anyone he hated more than Mufasa, it was his hairball of a nephew, Simba. If it weren't for him, Scar would be next in line for the throne.

Sensing Scar's anger, Zazu made a quick exit. "Story time begins promptly at sundown!" he called.

Scar leaped up, growling. What could be worse than being forced to entertain his nephew with a bedtime story? Unless . . .

Scar grinned as a positively wicked idea began to creep its way into his mind.

Scar crept over to the Elephant Graveyard. If his plan were going to work, he would need the help of the vicious hyenas who lived there.

"So let me get this straight," Shenzi said. "You want us to sneak into the lions' den and take the cub? With Mufasa right *there*?"

Scar smiled. "Leave Mufasa to me. He will be so distracted by my story, he won't even notice you!"

"That doesn't seem like the most foolproof idea," Banzai said.

"You want to eat, don't you?" Scar roared.

"We do!" Banzai cried.

"We enjoy eating," Shenzi said, slapping a giggling Ed.

"Well," Scar said, "once you steal the hairball away, you can have him."

By the time Scar and the three hyenas reached the Pride Lands, night had fallen.

"Now remember," Scar growled. "Listen closely to my story. I will let you know when and how to strike!"

Before the hyenas could reply, they heard the sound of voices coming toward them.

"Go!" Scar whispered as he spotted Mufasa and Simba rounding the corner.

"Scar," Mufasa said, "Simba and I were headed up to begin the storytelling."

"As was I," Scar replied quickly. "I think I've got a *very* good tale to tell, too."

Simba cocked his head. "Is it scary? I wanna hear something *really scary*. Not some boring story about an old king."

Scar knelt down, an evil glint in his eye. "The scariest."

"Cool!" Simba cried.

Soon the lions had gathered. Simba's friend Nala sat beside him. Across from them, Mufasa greeted the pride.

"Who would like to begin?" Mufasa asked.

"I would be honored to—" Zazu started.

"I'll go first," Scar interrupted, stepping forward.

Mufasa looked at his brother in surprise.

"He said he had a *really* scary story," Simba whispered to Nala.

"Very well," Mufasa said. "Scar, the floor is yours."

Scar took a deep breath and began: "Once upon a time, there lived a foolish king with many enemies." Scar glared down at Simba, who was hanging on his every word. "One night, the king decided to host a gathering. He invited animals from far and wide. This pleased the king's enemies. They knew the king would be distracted by his guests. This was their chance!

"The king's enemies invited some mighty elephants to the gathering. The elephants' feet were so large that they kicked up a large amount of dirt"—Scar scraped his large paws on the ground, creating a cloud of dust—"which made it difficult for the king and his subjects to see. It was the perfect opportunity to take the king without anyone noticing!"

Hearing their cue, the hyenas snuck toward the distracted lions, who were squinting at Scar through the haze. They had almost reached Simba when . . .

*"Ah-choo!"* Simba sneezed, diverting everyone's attention to him. The hyenas sprinted out of sight.

"Perhaps that's enough dust, Scar," Mufasa advised.

"Of course," Scar drawled, his eyes darkening.

"Unfortunately, things did not go as planned," Scar continued. "But no matter. The king's enemies soon came up with another plan. One night, when everyone was fast asleep, they snuck into the king's den, covered in mud. They were well disguised to blend with the surrounding rocks. When the king woke up, he did not know that his enemies were there with him."

He raised his voice pointedly. *"Right there with him. Disguised."*

"Is everything all right?" Zazu asked.

"Of course," Scar snapped. He took a deep breath, continuing his story as the hyenas—looking as though they had rolled around in the dirt and dust— inched toward Simba on their stomachs.

Suddenly, Mufasa stood up. The hyenas gasped at the sight of the mighty lion and made another hasty retreat.

Frowning, the king peered through the darkness. "Hmmm . . . I thought I heard something." He sat down again. "I apologize, Scar."

"Yes, well . . ." Scar went on, clearly agitated. "The enemies' second idea to sabotage the king did not work, either. So they had to resort to their third and final plan."

"Each day, the king stood on a great rock very similar to this one, and made announcements to his subjects."

"This is a very odd story," Zazu muttered.

"And so his enemies gathered at the *base* of the rock," Scar continued, ignoring the bird. "They climbed up one another until they reached a great height, until the enemy at the top was just high enough to reach the king's paws. And then . . ."

Scar paused as the hyenas climbed up to reach the space just beneath Simba.

"THEY POUNCED ON THE KING!" Scar bellowed.

The lions were startled, but Scar's outcry had also scared the hyenas! The three hyenas tumbled down the face of Pride Rock.

Out of the corner of his eye, Scar saw the dazed and bruised hyenas shuffle back toward the Elephant Graveyard. He sighed.

"What happened next?" Simba asked.

"Then the king swatted the enemies away," Scar said. "The end."

Simba looked disappointed. "Uncle Scar," he said, "that was a nice story, but maybe next time, you could make it scarier!"

**I**t was the end of the day at the arcade, and the video game characters were gathering in Game Central Station. Suddenly, all the lights in the station went out. It was a power outage!

"I think we're stuck," Wreck-It Ralph told his friend Vanellope von Schweetz. He was right. Until the power came back on, no one was going anywhere!

"Don't worry, everyone!" Fix-It Felix, Jr., called out. "My trusty hammer and I will have this fixed in no time!"

Ralph and Vanellope started to make their way toward Felix, but it
was hard to see without the lights.

"Come on, stink brain," Vanellope said. "I think I see a—*aaah!*"
Vanellope had run into someone!

"Oh! I'm s-sorry, Vanellope! I d-didn't see you there." It was Gene,
the Nicelander mayor from the *Fix-It Felix, Jr.* game.

"D-do you think the power will be out f-for a long time?" Gene asked Ralph and Vanellope nervously.

"I hope so!" Vanellope said. "This is fun!"

Vanellope started bouncing excitedly, but she stopped when she saw Gene shaking. "What's wrong, Gene?" Vanellope asked.

"The truth is," Gene said, "the idea of spending the night away from home scares me!"

Just then, Felix ran past with his hammer. "Felix, tap Gene with your hammer!" Ralph shouted. "Maybe then he won't be scared anymore."

Felix hit Gene lightly with his hammer. It was supposed to fix anything. The friends waited, but nothing happened. Gene was still scared.

"Sorry, Gene," Felix said sadly. "I guess there are just some things my hammer can't fix."

Vanellope and Ralph knew they needed to find a way to distract Gene until Felix could get the power back on.

"Are you thinking what I'm thinking, kid?" Ralph whispered to Vanellope.

"Absolutely!" Vanellope said. "Party! Come on, everyone! We're going to have a slumber party!"

"Wait, what? No!" Ralph said. He had definitely *not* been thinking about throwing a party.

"Trust me, big guy," Vanellope said, patting Ralph on the back. "I know what I'm doing." Then she climbed onto Ralph's shoulders and yelled, "Now let's have some fun!"

224

Ralph sighed. If there was one thing he knew about Vanellope, it was that once she got an idea in her head, there was no changing her mind.

Ralph looked around. "Satine," he called out, recognizing a fellow member of his Bad Guy support group, Bad-Anon. "Think you can help us out with some light?"

"It would be my pleasure," Satine said. He lit his staff, and a small circle of light filled the room.

The video game characters wasted no time in following Vanellope's lead. Soon they were all happily playing party games.

"Who knew that Zombie would be so good at this?" Ralph said, watching Zombie bob for apples.

But Gene wasn't paying any attention to Ralph. He was too busy wishing he was safe in his own bed.

"Come on, Gene," Ralph said, pushing his friend toward a limbo line. "You should give it a try!"

Gene took a deep breath and limboed under the pole. He could really bend!

"How's it going, Felix?" Ralph called to his friend.

Ralph looked around. Where *was* Felix?

"Up here, Ralph!" Felix called from within one of the ceiling vents high above Ralph. "Can't talk now! I think I'm getting close!"

Gene was having fun, but he was still worried. Vanellope needed another idea.

"It's time for charades!" she cried. "Gene, you keep time. Ralph, you're up first!"

"I don't know about this," Ralph and Gene said at the same time. Gene thought he'd be too scared to keep time, and Ralph didn't think he'd be very good at charades. But Vanellope wouldn't take no for an answer.

"Rooster? No. Ice cream? No. Giraffe? No. I got it, I got it, I got it. *Lollipop?*" Vanellope yelled as Ralph tried to act out the first word.

"Time's up!" Gene yelled.

"It's a cy-bug! I was trying to be a cy-bug!" Ralph explained.

Vanellope could see that Gene was starting to feel better. And she planned to keep him feeling that way! She grabbed Gene by the arm and dragged him toward the starting line for a three-legged race.

Gene glanced at Vanellope's fellow Sugar Rush racers. They looked tough. "Vanellope—maybe this isn't a good idea," he said.

"Come onnnn, Gene. We have to beat Taffyta and Candlehead!" Vanellope replied as she tied her leg to Gene's.

Before Gene could say another word, Sour Bill waved the starting

flag. The racers were off!

Taffyta and Candlehead quickly took the lead, with Wyntchell and

Duncan from the Bear Claw Brigade close behind.

"*Vanellope!*" Gene cried as he tried to keep up with her. "Slow down!"

"You slow down, you lose," Vanellope said. "Come on, Gene. You can

do it!"

Vanellope pulled Gene along as fast as she could, but they were still in third place.

Suddenly, one of the racers tripped! Everyone went flying—except for Vanellope and Gene. They raced into the lead and across the finish line in first place.

"You did it, Gene!" Ralph said, lifting Gene onto his shoulders.

"I did! I won!" Gene cheered loudly.

"Well, *we* won. But you were great!" Vanellope said.

"And look, you made it through the night!" Ralph said. He was right. The sun had come out! Suddenly, with a bang, Game Central Station lit up. Felix had fixed the power.

"I never thought I would make it through a whole night away from home," Gene said. "But now that I have, I guess it's not so scary after all. Thanks, guys!"

"Of course, buddy," Ralph said. "What are friends for?"

# The Queen's Spell

It was a beautiful fall day. Everyone in the kingdom was happily enjoying the crisp air and the bright orange and red leaves on the trees. Everyone, that is, except for the Queen.

"Where are the gloomy gray clouds?" she scowled as she watched some children playing in a pile of fallen leaves. "Where is the damp autumn rain? Where are the cold howling winds?"

Frustrated, the Queen stormed to her chambers to consult her Magic Mirror.

"Magic mirror on the wall, when will I see a gloomy fall?" she asked.

Purple smoke swirled, and a face appeared inside the mirror.

"Alas," the Magic Mirror replied, "I fear I see nothing but sunny skies."

"Curses!" the Queen cried, looking out the window. "No rain? Not a gray cloud to be seen? How can anyone stand all the cheer and happiness out there?"

"It is true the future is sunny and bright," the Magic Mirror continued, "but fear not, Your Majesty, for what exists can still be changed. Perhaps a spell could bring the gloom you seek."

"Of course!" the Queen said. "I shall use magic to chase away this cheerful weather."

The Queen hurried down the stairs to her secret chamber. It was full of old, dusty books and bottles of potions. She picked up one of her spell books.

"Gray . . . gloom . . ." she muttered as she flipped through the pages. Then she stopped. "Here it is! A spell for a frightful day."

The Queen read the list of ingredients out loud. "Three spiders, for gray skies and rain. Two rats' whiskers, for howling winds. And five shimmering scales from a snake, for thunder and lightning . . ."

The Queen pulled jar after jar from her shelves. Each one was empty. She had cast too many spells recently.

The Queen fumed, slamming an empty jar against the floor. How was she to get rid of the sun without the ingredients to cast her spell?

"I suppose I shall have to gather more," the Queen told herself. "Now, where would one find three spiders?"

The Queen's green eyes flashed as the answer came to her. "Of course! The well!"

The Queen marched upstairs, her dark cape swirling behind her. She pushed open the castle doors and stepped outside.

"Horrible sun!" she said, frowning at the bright light.

The Queen's mood lightened as she reached the well. She was, after all, quite fond of spiders. "Where are you, my lovelies?" she asked, peering into the dark well. "You love the dark dampness of the well. Where are you and your wonderful webs?"

The Queen searched the well, but she did not see any spiders. Instead, she found three ladybugs hanging from the bucket, getting a drink of water.

The Queen's face darkened. "So tiny! So cute!" she thundered.

Frightened, the three ladybugs quickly flew off.

As the Queen walked away, she didn't notice the single gray cloud that floated into the sky overhead.

Grumbling, the Queen looked at her list. "Rats!" she said. "That is what I need to find. A nice messy rat's nest with a rat inside."

At the edge of the woods, the Queen spotted an old oak tree. A pile of straw was sticking out from its gnarled roots. She walked to the tree and knelt down.

"Where are you, my lovely rats?" she asked. "Are you huddled here inside this messy nest? Come out and offer me your whiskers."

The Queen pushed aside the straw. But she did not see any rats. Instead, she saw two baby chipmunks taking a nap!

The Queen's face darkened. "So sweet! So cuddly!" she thundered.

At the sound of her voice, the baby chipmunks awoke. They quickly scampered out of the nest and up the tree trunk.

As the Queen stormed off, another gray cloud appeared in the sky.

"Curses! I shall never finish this spell!" the Queen complained. "The Magic Mirror will pay for sending me on this foolish errand."

As she started to head back toward the castle, the Queen spotted a hole in the ground.

"A snake's den!" she said hopefully, and she stopped. "Come on out, lovely snake. I need some of your scales."

A creature poked out its head. But it wasn't a snake. It was a bunny rabbit! Its adorable eyes widened in fright when it saw the Queen.

"So fluffy! So soft!" the Queen shouted, and the terrified bunny hopped away.

Angry, the Queen lifted her arms to the sky. "I can't find anything I need. Everything is too horribly cute!"

Her voice boomed like a clap of thunder. More dark clouds swept in, blocking the sunlight. The air suddenly grew cold.

*BOOM!* A real clap of thunder answered the Queen's voice. Lightning flashed and rain poured down from the clouds. For the first time all day, the Queen smiled.

"I did not need a silly spell at all!" she boasted. "It is gray and gloomy. My frightful day is finally here!"

But the Queen's bad mood was only strong enough to cause a short storm. After a minute, the rain lightened and then stopped completely. The clouds parted, and the sun shone through. Where the sunlight hit the moist air, a beautiful rainbow appeared in the sky!

"Noooooo!" the Queen shrieked.

Stomping her foot, she stormed back to her rooms in the castle.

"Magic mirror on the wall, tell me how to stop this all!" the Queen yelled at the Magic Mirror.

The face shimmered inside the mirror. "If Your Majesty desires gloom, then stay inside a darkened room," it replied.

"That is the most sensible thing you have said all day," the Queen snarled.

And so she stayed inside and sulked, leaving the cheerful fall day outside.

# Disney PRINCESS
# Sleeping Beauty
# A Message for Maleficent

**I**t was a time of celebration. King Stefan was getting married! He had chosen a kind princess from the neighboring kingdom to be his queen.

The king's subjects rejoiced. But no one was happier than the three good fairies, Flora, Fauna, and Merryweather. The three hurried to the castle to help the king and his future bride, Princess Leah, with the wedding plans.

Princess Leah had many ideas for her wedding. But she was new to the kingdom and did not know whom to invite. She wanted to make sure that no one in the kingdom was missed. So she asked the good fairies to make and deliver the invitations.

"Blue wedding invitations!" Merryweather said excitedly. "Can you think of anything lovelier?" With a flick of her wand, she created a large stack of blue envelopes.

"Oh, no, that won't do. They should be pink!" Flora said, changing the envelopes to a pale pink.

"Blue!" Merryweather said, changing them back.

Back and forth the envelopes went, until at last they settled on a light purple that both fairies had to agree was quite nice.

On the other side of the room, Fauna was hard at work on the guest list. "We don't need to invite too many people," she said thoughtfully. "Just the local royalty and noblemen. And all the king's subjects, of course. Oh, and every fairy, hedge witch, and wisewoman in a hundred-mile radius."

At Fauna's words, Flora looked up. "Do you think we should invite . . ." Her voice trailed off.

"Maleficent?" Merryweather asked quietly.

The fairy Maleficent lived high on the Forbidden Mountain. Her presence rarely brought any good cheer, but still, she *was* one of the king's subjects.

With a sigh, Fauna nodded. "I suppose we must," she said.

Merryweather shuddered. Just thinking about Maleficent gave her the shivers. "Who will we get to deliver the invitation?" she asked. "The way to Maleficent's castle is treacherous, and we cannot risk the invitation getting lost."

"One of us will have to go," Flora said. She flicked her hand and a dove appeared from her wand. It circled the room three times and then landed on Merryweather's shoulder. It was up to her to deliver the invitation to Maleficent!

The next day, Merryweather set off for Maleficent's castle. By evening she had reached the woods around the Forbidden Mountain. Her magic was weak here. She would have to walk.

Merryweather looked at a winding path that led into the woods.

It was getting dark, and the wind moaned eerily through the trees. Shivering, Merryweather pulled her wand out of her cloak pocket. With a flick of her wrist, she lit the tip of the wand. The warm light comforted her and she bravely continued on the path.

Alas, Merryweather was not alone in the woods. Maleficent's minions, the goons, were out patrolling. Even worse for poor Merryweather, the evil creatures loved causing mischief.

"I'll be there soon. Everything will be fine," Merryweather told herself as she tried to take her mind off the spookiness of the dark woods. But as she turned around a curve in the path, three of the goons jumped out at her.

Screaming, Merryweather ran down the path as fast as her little legs could carry her. Finally, she lost the goons.

"Those wicked creatures!" she said when she had calmed down. "I'd like to scare *them* and see how they'd like it!"

Merryweather looked around. Somehow, it seemed the woods had grown even darker. A cold wind blew through the trees, chilling the little fairy to the core. Merryweather wanted nothing more than to turn back, but the other fairies were counting on her.

As Merryweather made her way down the path, she noticed the trees growing closer and closer together. Large thorns stuck out from the trunks, making it impossible to get through without a scratch.

Suddenly, a chorus of loud howls echoed through the woods. It sounded like the cries were coming from right behind Merryweather!

"Oh, fiddlesticks!" she yelled as her cloak caught on a thorn. The goons had been bad enough. She certainly didn't want to meet any wolves in the dark woods.

Merryweather freed herself from the tree and hurried down the path as carefully as she could. The sooner she delivered the invitation, the sooner she could get back to the bright, warm castle.

Finally, Merryweather reached the edge of the woods. A giant stone staircase loomed above her, leading to Maleficent's lair.

Up, up, up Merryweather climbed until at last she came to a rickety bridge. On the other side was Maleficent's castle. Its jagged peaks rose into the sky, and a dark storm cloud circled overhead.

Merryweather looked
nervously at the bridge. It
looked like it could collapse
at any moment. Tucking
the invitation into her
cloak, she stepped
onto the bridge. The
wood shook and
creaked with every
step the little fairy took.
Merryweather kept her eyes
on the stone landing ahead
of her. Below her was a deep
chasm. If the bridge gave
out, she would have a
long way to fall.

Finally, Merryweather reached the other side. As she stepped onto the landing, a blast of green magic burst out of Maleficent's castle and a loud scream filled the air!

That was the last straw for Merryweather. She took out the invitation and carefully placed it on the castle's doorstep. Then, without looking back, she raced across the bridge, down the steps, and through the woods. She was so busy running away, she didn't see the goons who had been following her pick up the invitation and scamper off with it!

Merryweather didn't stop until she reached King Stefan's castle. She found Flora and Fauna in the great hall.

"Why, Merryweather, dear, whatever is the matter?" Flora asked.

"Maleficent had better come to this wedding," Merryweather said when she had caught her breath. "The journey to deliver that invitation nearly scared me to death!"

Flora smiled at Merryweather. "Come now," she said. "How bad could it really have been?"

Soon the day of King Stefan and Princess Leah's wedding arrived. Everyone in the kingdom gathered for the happy event. Everyone, that is, except for Maleficent.

From high on the Forbidden Mountain, the fairy looked down on the celebration. "Look at those fools," she said aloud. "Who do they think they are, not inviting me to their celebration? Well, enjoy it while you can. I'll get you for this . . . someday."

# One Brave Dug

**I**t was a dark and stormy night. The explorer Charles Muntz had gone to bed, but his faithful pack of dogs was still awake. Suddenly, a large flash of lightning lit up the sky.

"Oh! That was very bright," Dug said.

Across the room, Alpha, Beta, and Gamma huddled together. The three dogs hated storms—especially ones with scary lightning and thunder. But they would never admit that to Dug.

Just then, a loud rumble of thunder shook the airship. Beta and Gamma jumped. Beside them, Alpha cringed.

"Why isn't Dug scared?" Gamma whispered.

Alpha looked over at the golden retriever. "He's not smart enough to be scared," he said.

"Hey, Dug! Why aren't you scared of the storm?" Beta called.

Dug turned. "Should I be scared?" he asked. "Maybe I am! Thank you, my pack. You are helping me be a better Dug!"

Alpha smiled slyly. He was always looking for ways to get Dug in trouble, and he had just come up with a fantastic new plan.

"You seem to be enjoying the storm," Alpha told Dug. "That must mean you are a very brave dog."

"I am?" Dug said, lifting one ear and smiling. "You are Alpha and very smart. I will agree with you!"

"It's good that you are brave," Alpha continued. "Master told us that you should go outside to look for the bird. He thinks it might come out in this weather. The bird likes storms."

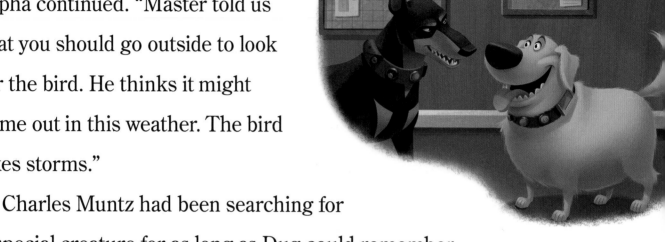

Charles Muntz had been searching for a special creature for as long as Dug could remember. Drawings of the birdlike animal filled every wall in their home.

Dug's eyes lit up. "Master has thought about me? And has given me a *mission*? I must leave at once!"

Gamma and Beta started laughing. "There's no way Dug won't be scared once he's outside in that storm!" Gamma said.

"Master will be so angry when he finds Dug gone!" Beta added.

"Alpha, this is your best idea yet," Gamma said. "I don't want to miss watching him get scared! Let's follow him!"

Dug bolted outside, eager to start his mission. Within seconds, his fur was soaked by the pouring rain and ruffled by the fierce wind.

"Find the bird. Find the bird. Master has given me a job to do. I must not let him down!"

Dug was so focused on finding the creature that he didn't notice Alpha, Beta, and Gamma trailing behind him.

At the edge of the jungle, Dug paused. The trees cast long shadows and hid the moon and stars from sight. Dug continued on. "The dark is very quiet," he said.

Suddenly, Dug heard rustling coming from the trees. Looking up, he saw countless pairs of giant glowing eyes watching him.

Far behind Dug, Alpha, Beta, and Gamma saw the glowing eyes, too. *"Aaah!"* the three screamed. "WHAT ARE THOSE? SCARY EYES!"

Dug moved around to the moonlit side of the tree. Looking up, he saw that the eyes belonged to a group of fruit bats munching happily on some fruit!

"Hello!" Dug said. "You are not the bird. You are bats! You must be able to see very far from up there. Have you seen the bird?"

Alpha breathed a sigh of relief. "They're just fruit bats," he said. He was glad the eyes didn't belong to anything *really* scary.

Gamma was not so calm. He cowered beside Beta, covering his eyes. "Are they gone? Are they gone?"

Alpha scowled. He had expected Dug to be scared, but instead the golden retriever seemed *happy*!

The rain was still pouring down, but Dug didn't mind. Wishing the bats well, he continued on his way.

Dug had not gone far when he felt something small and slimy brush past his leg. "Something is on the ground near my leg," Dug said. "I wonder what it could be."

Behind Dug, Beta jumped into the air as something slimy bumped against his leg, too. "Snake!" he cried. "It's going to get me! It's going to wrap itself around me and squeeze me tight and—"

"Shhh!" Alpha whispered. "Quiet! What is the *matter* with you?"

Just then, lightning flashed, and Dug saw that he was standing beside a rushing creek. A family of frogs was happily jumping past him toward the slick rocks.

"Hello! You are frogs," Dug said. "You are splashing about. You look like you are having fun. I am having fun, too. I am looking for the bird. Perhaps you have seen it?"

But the frogs just kept hopping along.

As Dug walked deeper into the jungle, he heard leaves rustle on the path ahead of him.

"*Squirrel!*" Dug cried, turning toward the sound.

Dug looked around, but he didn't see anything. "I was mistaken. There is nothing there," he said.

Putting his nose to the ground, Dug kept going. Soon he came to a big clearing. On the far side, he thought he saw a tall, thin shadow moving in the darkness at the mouth of a cave.

Dug bounded across the clearing to investigate, wagging his tail eagerly. "Find the bird! Find the bird! Find the bird!"

Behind him, Alpha, Gamma, and Beta crept toward the edge of the clearing. They were cold, tired, and frustrated.

"Great idea, Alpha," Beta complained. "We've spent the whole night roaming around the jungle getting soaked, and the only one who's been scared is Gamma, by a bunch of harmless fruit bats!"

"No, I wasn't!" Gamma replied. "Besides, *you* were scared of a bunch of tiny frogs!"

"You are *both* scaredy-dogs!" Alpha hissed at them. "There is nothing to be scared—Wait! Look!" The dogs turned in time to see Dug enter the dark cave.

"Dug is sure to be scared in there!" Beta said. "Or lost for good!"

Suddenly, a huge bolt of lightning flashed across the sky,
illuminating the clearing. Through the rain, the dogs saw a horrible
fearsome-looking shadow standing at the mouth of the cave!

"*Aaaah!*" Alpha shouted. "It's a monster! Run for your life!"

Alpha, Beta, and Gamma turned on their heels and dashed through
the jungle, back toward the safety of the blimp.

Alpha's screams got Dug's attention. "Oh, it is my pack!" he said. "They must have been worried about me. They know how important my mission is and came to help. They are the best friends a Dug could ever have."

Dug tilted his head to one side. "I wonder where they are going."

From the mouth of the cave, Dug saw that the rain had slowed and the sun was rising. Its rays broke through the rain clouds, creating a breathtaking rainbow.

"The sun is rising!" Dug said. "That is why they are running! Master will be awake soon! I must go back and report."

"Beta! Gamma! Alpha!" Dug shouted when he got home. Looking around the airship, Dug saw that the rest of his pack was not there. "My pack must still be outside. I will wait for them."

Just then, Muntz walked into the room.

"Master!" Dug said. "You are awake! I must tell you all about my mission!"

"What mission?" Muntz snapped. "What are you talking about? And where are the rest of the dogs?"

Dug smiled at his master. "They are outside!"

"What?" Muntz shouted. "They went out in *that* weather? Crazy dogs. The thunder must have scared them silly, and they'll be drenched from the rain. Ooooh, they are in so much trouble when they get back. I swear . . ."

Muntz shook his head and looked down at Dug. "Come on," he said. "Let's get the day started.  I'll deal with those silly dogs later. Bet you they got themselves—"

"*Lost!* We're *lost*!" Gamma cried.

The dogs were cold, wet, and terrified. And to make matters worse, the rain had washed away their footprints! They had no idea how to get home!

"Great idea, Alpha," Beta grumbled. "Let's give Dug a mission to scare him! Get him in trouble with the master! But look at us! WE ARE THE ONES WHO ARE LOST!"

"Would you please shut your mouth?" Alpha barked. "Keep looking for our footprints! That's the only way we'll ever get home!" He hung his head. "Master will be so displeased with us when he finds us gone! This is all Dug's fault!"

# Monsters

# The Spooky Sleepover

**I**t was a quiet morning at Monsters, Inc. James P. Sullivan was looking over the monthly laugh reports. Sulley was the president of Monsters, Inc. Suddenly, the phone rang.

"Hello?" Sulley said.

"It's dispatch," said the voice on the other end of the line. "Annual slumber party at little Shannon Brown's house. Waxford is out sick. We need a replacement."

Sulley thought about whom to send. He wanted to put his best monster on the case. He smiled to himself. Who better for the job than his friend Mike Wazowski? Mike could make anyone laugh, and he was the top Laugh Collector at Monsters, Inc.

Sulley knew his best friend would be the perfect choice.

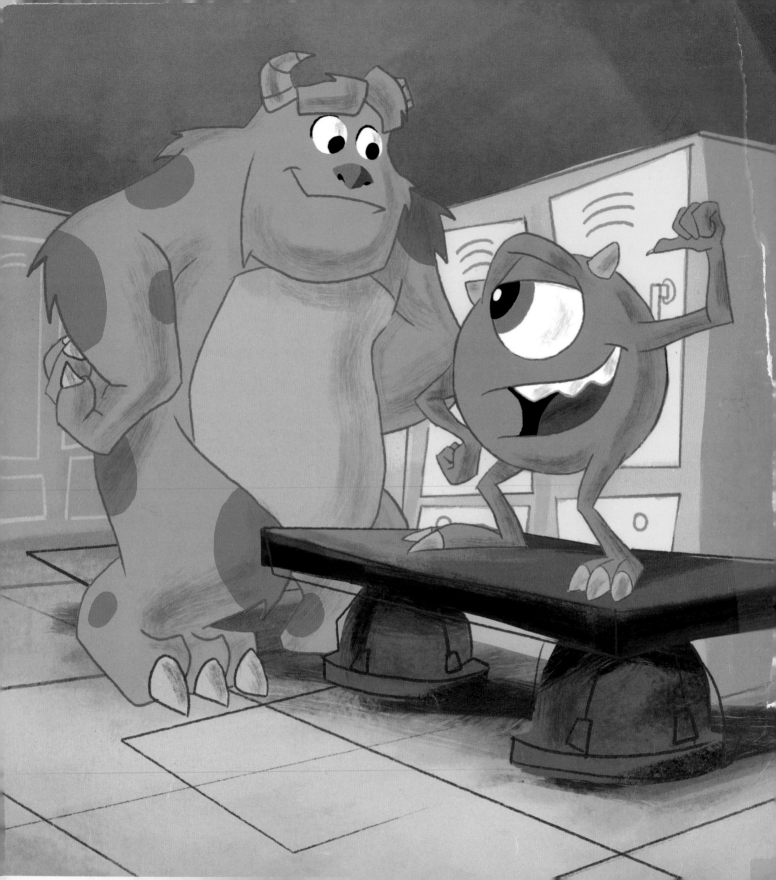

Mike was in the locker room getting ready for work when Sulley walked in and explained the situation.

"I'm your man," Mike said confidently.

"Great!" Sulley exclaimed. Whistling, he went back to his office to finish his laugh reports.

"A room full of kids? Collecting laughs will be a piece of cake," Mike said as a door slid into his station on the Laugh Floor.

Mike opened the door and walked through the closet into Shannon Brown's room. It was empty.

"Hello?" Mike called. He looked around and peeked under the bed—but there was no one there. Just as Mike started walking toward the closet, he heard laughter.

"All right, now we're talking!" Mike said. "Kids, prepare to roll with laughter."

Just then, a flash of lightning lit up the dark room and thunder cracked across the sky. Mike jumped. If there was one thing that scared him, it was thunderstorms! Job or no job, he was getting out of there!

Mike raced back to the closet. But when he opened the door, he was standing in a normal closet, not the Laugh Floor.

Mike realized that the lightning must have broken the door. He knew that he needed to find the slumber party and another closet door—fast.

Heading into the dark hallway, Mike tried to follow the sound of laughter. The floor creaked spookily beneath him.

Mike stopped and looked around.

The wall was covered in creepy paintings of people, and they all seemed to be staring right at him!

"I've got to get out of here," Mike muttered to himself. Then he saw something that made him freeze in his tracks!

Sitting at the end of the hall was a large furry creature with fangs. Thinking the creature was a fellow monster, Mike started to walk closer, relieved. Suddenly, the creature jumped on him, knocking him down. It wasn't a monster; it was a dog!

*"Ahhhh!"* Mike screamed. He hated dogs. Mike pushed the dog off himself and ran into a nearby room, then slammed the door shut. He was safe—for now!

Meanwhile, Sulley was working on the Laugh Floor.

"Sulley! Sulley!" the floor manager shouted, running over. "Mike still hasn't returned from the slumber party."

When Sulley checked the door, he found it wasn't working. Mike was trapped!

Sulley didn't like the idea of Mike being stuck in Shannon's house. He needed to fix the door—*now*! He quickly brought in a maintenance crew. Together, the monsters tried to get it to open properly. But nothing worked.

Sulley and the monsters decided to try getting into Shannon's house using a new door. Finally, it made a clicking sound. It worked! Now the door would open into a different room in the house!

Back in the house, Mike opened another door. It led to the bathroom.

As Mike searched for the light switch, he tripped on a yellow rubber ducky. "Ouch!" he said as he went rolling across the floor like a ball. Finally, Mike crashed into the wall and came to a stop.

Sudden, he heard giggling from down the hall.

Mike did not like this assignment—or this house. But as long as he was stuck there, he was determined to find the party. Lifting himself off the floor, he followed the laughter to a door. But when he opened it, the room was quiet.

Slowly, Mike entered the dark, silent room. All of a sudden, a light
came on! Mike jumped. Shannon Brown and all her friends roared with
laughter! They thought Mike looked funny sneaking into the room.

*"Ahhhhhhhhh!"* Mike was so scared that he couldn't stop yelling.

At that moment, the closet door opened and Sulley burst into the room. When he heard Mike screaming, he started screaming, too. Mike jumped up into Sulley's arms.

The girls at the slumber party laughed even harder. A big blue monster with purple spots hugging a little green one-eyed monster was one of the funniest things they had ever seen.

Mike and Sulley smiled at each other. Then Mike jumped to the floor, and they both took a bow. The kids cheered.

"Looks like our work here is done," Sulley said with a smile.

He and Mike headed through the closet door and back to the Laugh Floor. They had filled so many canisters with laughs that Mike was named the top Laugh Collector that day.

"I was never scared for a second," Mike said, hoping Sulley would believe him.

"Me neither, buddy," Sulley replied, his big furry fingers crossed behind his back. "Me neither."